Little Did We Know:

Making the Write Impression

Bernadette Adora
Mary Lou Edwards
Carolyn B Healy
Ellie Searl

Designed by Ellie Searl

ISBN: 978-0-578-00298-9

www.writeimpressions.blogspot.com

Write Impressions Press
LaGrange, Illinois

Dedicated To . . .

. . . three good and absolutely
wonderful women – this has been
a marvelous ride!
And, to Candace – one daughter in
a million, who has earned the right
to follow her bliss.
Bernadette

. . . George and Lia who, with
equanimity and grace, are always
there to read the roughest of drafts.
Mary Lou

. . . my team - you know who you are.
Carolyn

. . . Ed and Katie – your wisdom and
insight are spot-on.
Ellie

Four
Voices

We Are . . .

    . . . writers determined to explore what makes us tick, have the last word, savor the forbidden apple, and then come back for more.

Bernadette Adora, a longtime Chicagoan, loves her city and all that it has come to represent. She fancies herself a storyteller not unlike her father's people, who hailed from the hills of Kentucky. Born and raised on Detroit's Westside, she has been shaped by the working-middle class of Chicago and Detroit. Growing up in the fifties and sixties, Bernadette was strongly influenced by the Civil Rights Movement and the music of Motown, a rich mixture of dreams and reality. Using the written word, she continually explores and weaves together the various threads handed down to her by strong-minded and complex women, who raised, guided, and continuously gave Bernadette permission to be HerSelf.

Mary Lou Scalise Edwards is a Chicagoan born into an Italian-American family with all the blessings and liabilities that encompasses. Raised a Union Maid, Mary Lou was a born organizer who believes people not only have the right, but also the responsibility, to speak up even when their voices shake. Fortunately for the reader, Mary Lou's voice never falters. Her comic take on life's absurdities captures painful and outrageous truths, which cut deeply into our modern psyche. Her take-no-prisoners style exposes the guilty and gives voice to the wounded.

Carolyn B Healy is a therapist-turned-writer who has invested hundreds of hours listening to people as they rewrite their life stories. While her interests include serious things like grief, resilience and transformative change, her vantage point allows her to address them with insight and a certain dark humor. A lifelong Chicagoan, she grew up the only child of a single mom, which fueled her curiosity about how other people live, and strengthened her backbone. She has been a columnist for her local newspaper and is writing a book on finding the hidden gifts in grieving.

Ellie Volckmann Searl began telling stories as soon as she could talk. The splendor of the Adirondack Mountains and Lake Champlain seeped into her being, as did the rhythms of small-town life. Her storytelling now draws inspiration from the richness of her experiences and the diverse personalities she's encountered while living, working, and raising a family in New York, Delaware, Vermont, Quebec, Ohio, and Illinois. Ellie is passionate about justice, equality, and freedom of the spirit. She taught the art of writing to Chicagoland middle-schoolers, whose curiosity, energy, and enthusiasm for life gave her insight into the dreams of the sometimes disregarded. Ellie writes of everyday quirkiness, getting to the heart of life's yearnings, ambiguities, and idiosyncrasies.

CONTENTS

ARE WE HAVING FUN YET?

HOMESPUN

POCKETBOOK POWER PROSPERITY

SAVOR THE MEMORIES

THE ART OF ASKING

LETTING GO

Are We Having Fun Yet?

This Was Supposed . . .

     . . . to be a blast - - a good time, we said. We'd share the burden of the blog. No one would get stuck, no deadlines, no pressure - - just fun memories, crazy stories, whatever was on our minds.

NOT A PERMANENT SOLUTION
Mary Lou Edwards

I wonder, if in the Land of Make Believe, these baby dolls have flashbacks about their first permanent wave. I know mine was seared into my brain. I was about to start first grade. Apparently neither the nightly ritual of winding endless banana curls on my fidgety noggin nor my non-stop whining about stupid boys yanking on my braids was appealing to my mother, so her cousin Della the beautician's suggestion of a hot perm seemed like the perfect solution.

Though I viewed the horrendous contraption with its black wire tentacles and gleaming steel curler clamps with great trepidation, my mom said I'd be too busy reading books to waste time on the nightly hair-setting ritual. This permanent, she promised, would end my hairy tales of woe; I'd be permanently beautiful.

It took hours to section my massive mane into appropriate sized chunks for the electric curlers. Only the promise of a fuchsia hair ribbon forced me to sit still atop two giant Chicago telephone directories. Finally a disgusting permanent wave solution was applied to each curler, and Della threw the switch. Immediately my head started hissing and steaming like a pot of boiling ravioli. With her eyes as big as the giant meatballs my Nonna fried on Sunday morning, my mother asked, "Della, is her head supposed to smoke like that?"

"That's only steam," said Della. "If her hair was burning, we'd smell it—singed hair smells disgusting."

Looking at my mother's popping eyeballs and smelling the stinking fumes sent me into orbit. My sotto sobs erupted into what would have been hair raising shrieks had not my head been so wired.

"This is an electric chair!" I screamed. "I'm turning into Frankenstein!"

My mother grabbed the telephone book highchair.

"Sit still," she hissed. "If you fall off those phone books, you'll be scalped like an Indian and you'll have to wear a babuschka to school. Besides," she grinned, "you told me you wanted to be beautiful!"

That was true. I did want to be beautiful. I settled down.

A few minutes later the wires were disconnected, the hair unwound, and a nauseating "neutralizer" was sloshed through my ringlets. Then my locks were twisted into pin curls, and I was placed under a giant steel helmet for another hour to dry.

At last my tresses were combed out with the coveted fuchsia bow planted in the massive eagle's nest of curls.

I was beautiful.

Two weeks later my hair was stick straight. The beauty maven said the "hot wave" didn't take; she would give me a "cold wave."

"No, no," I told my mother, "No, thanks! No more torture. Being beautiful is way too much trouble." And so it was and it is…

MY AMAZING METAMORPHOSIS
Carolyn B Healy

As a therapist, I've been in the business of change for a long time and have learned to distrust the quick turn, the sudden conversion. It is too good to be true, and you know how that usually turns out.

The actor goes on a racist rant and suddenly is moved to meet with civil rights leaders to make the world a better place? The prospective bride or groom suddenly turns in the religion of their youth for a more convenient one so they can get on with the ceremony? I smell expediency.

Instead, I believe in slow, grinding change, the kind that takes place when rivers wear down rocks. The kind that has finally happened to me.

I grew up on the South Side of Chicago, a non-Irish, non-Catholic only child. I didn't meet the profile. I needed some way to belong. When friends began to veer even further away from me into movie magazines and home permanents, I found my niche. I became a White Sox fan.

I chose Luis Aparicio as my hero, Number 11. I bought a white sweatshirt and painstakingly sewed his name and number on the back using bias tape, and wore it to every game I could talk my mother into attending, always with several friends in tow.

We would wait outside the fence after the games, angling for autographs. One winter, I subscribed to the St. Louis Sporting

News, and scoured every issue for news of Little Looie and his teammates. I had it bad.

And then came the 1959 season and the pennant. I was in heaven. I spent all my babysitting money on a transistor radio with an earphone that would allow me to hear every minute of every game.

Our defeat at the hands of the hated Dodgers took a lot out of me. I hung in for the next few years, but then the waves of adolescence took my attention to other matters and I virtually stopped reading the sports page, a fallen-away fan.

Once I embarked on a mixed marriage with a life-long Cubs fan, I didn't do much to hold up my end of the debate. I was a little puzzled at the vehemence of my new relatives' feelings on the matter, but was sure they'd feel better once they racked up a pennant of their own, which was bound to happen soon.

In the meantime, I watched the occasional game and developed a lasting affection for the endless optimism and lack of bitterness in Cub nation. No matter how painfully disappointed the fans were by the end of the season, every spring they came back for more, year after year. Their glass remained half-full.

And that's all I noticed until last week, when I was watching the Cubs-Sox game on ESPN with my never-wavering husband. In fact, he noticed it before I did.

"You're rooting for the Cubs?" he said.

"Oh, I guess I am," I said. "Wow."

Now, that is real change – when it sneaks up and surprises you, when it descends on you without being summoned. Sorry, Sox, I've gone over the fence.

END GAME
Bernadette Adora

I do not pretend to know the strategies that make up the game of chess; I'm far too right-side-of-the-brain to care much about it all. But, I comprehend the basic rules of the game and follow instructions fairly well, so years ago I took a little time to learn the game of chess, and I play a little on the computer. It's far easier that way since I'm a person who remains stuck at the beginner's level with absolutely no interest in progressing further – at least not in virtual-time.

To be honest, my interest in the game of chess is more visual if not tactile; I like the game of chess as a thing of beauty that can bring together the senses of sight, touch, and smell. The feel of natural stone or wooden pieces carved and rubbed smooth, with edges rounded, sitting atop a sleek board – this is what pleases me the most. I like to describe it as the game of chess in relative-time.

For one who has reduced the game of chess to an easy and simple pleasure, it came as a surprise to me more than anyone when I learned that I play the game of chess each and every day in earnest. There are days, sometimes weeks, that I play several games simultaneously only to arrive at the end game with the board overturned and pieces flying in righteous indignation. I call this the game of chess in real-time.

There is a fellow with whom I work; he helps me, I help him, and together we try and help everyone else make sense of the world when it starts going sideways rather than straight ahead. Recently, he told me that most men just muddle through when it comes to their relationships with women. And I was just being told this! Later, I thought about what he said and wondered if I had stumbled onto this information years sooner would I have had fewer expectations, more patience, better ------ not! Let me stop myself right here. I already have a huge problem with seeing the potential in nearly every person I meet rather than seeing the "deal." Not unlike that old school (no pun intended), special ed teacher I've admired, I see good and talented souls, who, with a little hard work and a whole lotta love, can be all that they hope to be, if not more. That part is important, please don't gloss over: "if not more." However, and this is a big, HOWEVER, I've recently come to understand that each and every one of us is simply muddling through.

Right-side or left-side, the game of chess is a real-life phenomenon in real-time for too many of us. New thought thinkers point to ego, point to fear, point to illusion, point and then point some more as I, along with others, continue with the game of chess. All the while, promising to disengage only to engage again.

At this stage of my life, I have gotten tired of playing the game of chess in real-time, particularly with those of the opposite sex. I am bone weary of the end game and all my misplaced stuff that comes along with it. I just want to cease muddling through, turn a beautifully carved piece gently over on its side, take a few deep breaths, gaze at the man sitting across from me, and recognize him not as an opponent but rather as an extension of my weary boned self -- smile truly, reach over, and gently touch his hand and lovingly suggest that he and I remain present. I want to hear, as we stand up together and move away from the board, about his joys and no more about his sorrows; I want to hear about his hopes and no more about his fears; I want to hear about his today and no more about his yesterdays, and then I want to be invited and welcomed to share the same. I want to be able to savor each instance of sitting still, of standing, of moving alongside "he," whom I now recognize as being a part of "me," who together transforms momentarily into a "we." In my imagining, the end game is just that – an end to the game now transformed into a myriad of new beginnings, new possibilities that flow together moment to moment --- yes, even in real-time.

WHAT ABOUT ME?
Ellie Searl

He leaned against the center column of the kitchen porch and looked at me with that forlorn, Eeyore pout. His glass eye roved off to the left while the other one welled up with tears. "What about me? What's going to happen to me?"

He shuffled to his Barcalounger and slumped into the sanctuary of sculpted dents. Years of lethargy had molded creases into the grey vinyl upholstery, shaping the dirt-encrusted plastic into the exact contours of his body. The solace of familiarity didn't ease his distress. He leaned his head back into the depression of the top cushion and moaned.

I never quite understood why Dad wanted his recliner on the kitchen porch. We owned elegant, though aged, white ladder-back rockers and wicker chairs, which graced the wide, covered veranda on the side of the house overlooking the lake. But Dad wanted to sit with his scotch-on-the-rocks and watch traffic in comfort, even though there wasn't much traffic to watch. An occasional car tumbled out of the mountain road beyond our house and sailed down the hill to the village. Farmers in rusty pick-ups tipped their hats, and truckers hauling silage honked. If Dad were in a good mood, he'd lift his drink, spilling his cheap scotch on his pants. If not, he'd bellow, "Slow down! Quit kicking up our gravel!"

One summer evening, while the family attempted small talk over cocktails, an out-of-towner stopped just beyond our property line to admire the orange and purple sunset, the colors shifting and slicing through the mountains past our meadows. "What's he doing? His tires are on the edge of our grass. He's just trying to make me mad." And then the excruciatingly familiar suffering sigh: a belabored intake of breath through clenched teeth, followed by a slow, heavily grunted exhale. An exaggerated swig of his drink exhibited finality to the event, like an exclamation point giving authority to his pronouncement

A 'Fred testimonial' was meant for us to take notice, and it demanded a response. If none came, there was a 'Fred coda,' which took the shape of a loud "Hmmm?" as in "Don't you agree?" Nobody did. Eventually someone broke the silence and tried to show reason, which was actually appeasement: conciliatory comments to mollify Dad until his scotch could kick in and he'd fall asleep in front of TV after dinner. But in our heads, the small talk became big thoughts - big with stress, big with anger, big with resentment - thoughts that each of us had and shared in private but never dared say out loud in front of our father, or mother, for that matter. At moments like these Mom had her own excruciatingly familiar sigh, only hers was shallow and slightly sing-songy, as though she had just seen a baby bird fall out of its nest – a helpless, pervasive sigh. But true to form, she'd fake a laugh and say something witty to lift the melancholy that hung over us like a sunset gone to seed.

Dad had a college degree in civil engineering; he was a skilled land surveyor; he showed artistic ability in oil painting, sketching, map-making, and embroidery. He cultivated beautiful gardens with lush string beans, sweet beefsteak tomatoes, and exceedingly huge zucchini. He enjoyed baking bread and making German spaetzle noodles with sauerbraten, and in the summer, he'd husk corn. So what happened?

Dad was a personal contradiction wrapped in a heavy-set, six-foot, three-inch bulk of a man, whose central belief of life and how it should treat him stopped developing when he was in those self-centered teenage years of supreme narcissism. At sixteen, the *Me First* syndrome is expected and humored. At any age beyond twenty-five, exhibiting childish, self-absorbed behaviors is an embarrassment. Dad was stuck in the expectations of teenage-ness, looking toward others to fill his bottomless happiness glass. That's it. Mostly he just liked to be waited on.

For Dad, being waited on meant guessing what he wanted and getting it for him before he knew he wanted it. His adolescent self reared its head during these gimme gimme episodes. There was hell to pay if Dad saw someone with a treat and his TV tray was empty. "Is that ice cream?" He'd ask in his half-sleep, half-sober whine. Then came the follow-up grievance call. "Can't a guy get a dish of ice cream around here?" Not a proper request that showed a touch of respect, but a command designed to corral the nearest family member into action. When it was my turn, I addressed the situation in silence: stomach in knots, head pounding, face twisted, and hands scooping ice cream into a bowl for the head of the family lazing torpidly in the beige, tufted den recliner while he watched TV with one glazed eye and yelling "Oh, for Pete's sake," if the music got too loud.

When the world behaved properly for Dad, life for the rest of us paced along smoothly. So, to the extent that we could, my two older brothers and I provided opportunities to orchestrate good cheer and lighthearted humor, no matter how emotionally counterfeit the efforts. Pretense was a matter of course. "Make him laugh, and keep us happy." That's how we functioned. We complimented his freshly grown vegetables. We oohed and aahed over his homemade bread, spaetzles, and sauerbraten. We made dinner table jokes that corresponded with something he liked. The jokes became traditions. Dinner was calm if we had rice. "Rice is nice." Dad was particularly partial to that one. It matched a rice commercial that made him laugh, and referring to it meant we cared about him. So simple, yet so therapeutic.

Peace at the dinner table took an ugly turn when the phone rang, or the meat was tough, or my brother's best friend, Tim, came to the kitchen door. "Why the hell does he always have to show up at supper time?" Then, stomach in knots, head pounding, face twisted, and hand clenched onto my fork, I'd finish my meal in agitated silence. Dad sighed his insufferable big sighs, Mom sighed her pathetic little sighs, and my brothers and Tim ate dinner in the den.

Children aren't equipped to understand or analyze their parents' behaviors. I knew Dad had a terrible accident during a wood chopping incident in his early thirties when an errant piece of tree bark flew into his left eye, blinding it instantly. Dad occasionally complained about his lack of depth perception, but other than that, I never gave his eye much thought. I was used to it. I also knew that Dad was an only child who had been doted upon by his mother and bullied by his father.

Perhaps Dad's disgruntled behavior was due to his ill-fated, debilitating experience. Or perhaps he lingered in those coddled, yet overlooked, only-child stages of youth, still expecting a mother to ease his troubles and still craving approval from a domineering father.

Whatever the reason, he was helpless. Dad couldn't meet the ordinary challenges of finding fulfillment or gratification in everyday occurrences. He couldn't overcome the all-encompassing hopelessness that continued throughout his lifetime - a lifetime spent drinking scotch, earlier and earlier each day, letting his garden wither and his artwork dwindle. Did he ever notice that he had three beautiful children, a generous wife, and a great deal of talent? Did he know he became an unlovable man?

When I still lived at home, I never confronted him – ever. I was too afraid – afraid of his intermittent love-hate affair with the world he built around him and us. Afraid of his unpredictability. Afraid of his ambiguous, yet omnipresent disapproval that interrupted the equilibrium I tried to manage in his presence.

And so at his worn-out age of seventy-eight he wanted to know what would become of him. How would he manage? There he sat in that hideous lounge chair, swirling his scotch, spilling it on his pants, looking pitifully at the porch floor boards wondering who would take care of him now that Mom had her arm in a sling because she ripped her rotator cuff playing golf. What a sad sight. He'd never change.

But I had. I had found courage. No stomach knots. No head poundings. Nothing clenched. Just a few words forming along with a twisted smile. I couldn't resist.

"Lighten up, Dad. You still know how to pour your own scotch."

I turned and walked into the kitchen, letting the screen door slam behind me. I have no idea if he sighed or what he said, if anything. It didn't matter.

Homespun

The Fabric of Our Lives . . .

   . . . is woven from gossamer thread experiences, knitted observations, and knotted memories. These fibers are the rough and the smooth, the warp and the weft, that make up the patterns of our lives.

NO LONGER WORTH LIVING?
Carolyn B Healy

I slid into the pew. It was a Tuesday night and I went alone. There were about twenty of us, an assortment of silver-haired elders with a smattering of younger people like me, one still dressed for the office, most more casually, as if they'd stopped in on the way to the grocery store. Each of us carefully avoided eye contact with the others.

In the back, a table was covered with tall stacks of pamphlets available for a small fee, "The Right to Die," "Special Issues in Alzheimer's Disease," and other titles. The stacks were so high that it suggested a miscalculation – either another hundred or so people had been expected, or each of us was to grab multiple copies to pass out to our friends and neighbors. In either case, it made the evening seem like a failure before it even began.

The three speakers whispered together in the back of the room, watching the clock. At exactly seven-thirty, the tall lanky mid-forties man in jeans and a plaid shirt strode to the front, while his colleagues slipped into seats in the first row.

He discussed the founder, a British journalist who had assisted his wife, at her request, to end her suffering from bone cancer by brewing her coffee laced with deadly medications. When his career later brought him to the States, he and several others, including his second wife, founded the Society in 1980 in his garage in California, to bring the "hopelessly ill" news of their right to practice "self-deliverance" and of methods to achieve "hastened death."

The next speaker was the stocky kindly-looking woman, gray-haired and dressed like Kathy Bates in *Misery*. Her voice was strong as she presented the public affairs angle. As she covered court rulings, right-to-die legislation and subsequent legal challenges, her outrage grew. She spoke against the restraints on people who simply wanted to determine their own time and manner of death, and the penalties for those who might assist them.

When she got to the part about famous snuff-meister Dr. Jack Kevorkian, the defrocked doctor who claimed to have assisted 120 people to die, her conviction that he was a martyr to the cause leaked out among her facts. The first death he helped accomplish was a fifty-four year old woman who had Alzheimer's. His last was a lethal injection provided in 1999 to a fifty-two year old accountant with ALS, which led to his conviction for second degree murder.

I set the pamphlets down next to me to give me some distance from heroes who bring death to your door. I had a client once whose religion taught that bad spirits attach themselves to objects, and won't go away until the objects are discarded, or better yet, destroyed. The issue that had brought her to counseling was guilt and anguish that had plagued her for months after the end of an illicit relationship. She proved her theory - all her symptoms evaporated as soon as she burned the notes and trinkets left over from her lover. If she was right, these pamphlets might sweep forces into my life I wouldn't be able to control.

The third speaker, the calm man dressed in chinos and a buttoned-down shirt, outlined the practical assistance system. The wanting-to-die person, while still of sound mind and body, explains his reasons for wanting to end it all. If he passes muster, convincing them of his seriousness and emotional health, he is assigned a guide, a volunteer who promises to stick with him throughout the course of his illness, continuing to discuss the conditions of mind and body and intention. The Society becomes the last matchmaker you'd ever need.

Questions bombarded me. Who are these people, these guides? Survivors of a parent's excruciating death by cancer? Anarchists looking for the cracks in the social order? Well-meaning humanitarians? Libertarians looking to kick government out of our personal business? Does it even matter what their motives are, as long as the person who wants to die gets to? Is wanting to die enough?

The lecturer, a serene man who wouldn't worry you a bit if he sat next to you on the subway, laid out the long-recommended method of – well, since they refused to call it suicide– hastened death: a particular cocktail of medications that could easily be prescribed by a sympathetic doctor over time and stockpiled for the final day. They would then be crushed and mixed into applesauce which the individual could feed himself. If he could feed himself.

A newer method was gaining support as well, he explained, that involved helium and a plastic bag over the head, secured with rubber bands or panty hose. The hope was that this method would provide a reduced chance of unintended survival.

Had the woman sitting next to me sucked in her breath at that revelation, or was that me? There seemed to be too little air in the room, too little movement to account for twenty-some living creatures.

As one who has spent a career trying to stand between suicidal people and their permanent solutions to temporary problems, I had negotiated dozens of deals, even written them down so my client could sign them, "no harm contracts" they are called: "I won't act on a suicidal impulse unless I call you/go to the ER/ call the hotline." What an optimistic endeavor, to make rational agreements with people subject to irrational and overpowering impulses. I sometimes wondered if I helped keep people alive by tipping them off to how devastated I would be if they did kill themselves. Maybe the point is to know that someone cares that you are still here, that your counselor is awake at two a.m. hoping that you haven't pulled the trigger.

But this, it began to dawn on me, was entirely different. These people had permanent problems, terminal ones. It also became clear to me that while the suicide decisions that I had tried so hard to prevent can teeter on thousands of precarious and temporary impulses, the decision necessary to a end a life as the Society laid it out is made day after day, over a period of time, and involves planning and long-lasting intention. And courage. And help.

My neighbor offered me a mint. I accepted. A few audience members spoke of their own situations – a spouse with a painful disease, a parent who had asked their help – most did not.

Meanwhile, across town, my mother sat, watched over by assisted care staff. She was at once no longer herself, yet unmistakably and indelibly who she had always been, in the moments when she would still surprise me with a joke or gaze at me with undiluted love. When on earth would her moment have been, when she would have thrown in the towel, declared her life no longer worth living? Should I have asked her that? We were certainly past it now, a relief of sorts.

She would have been, I told myself, of two minds: she would support the right of a person not to live out her days in dependency and diminishing faculties. But she was also one to let things run their natural course. She would survive as long as she could because life was good and she was part of it. Realizing that, I could breathe easier.

As I stood to go, I looked again at my neighbor and smiled.

"Good night, dear," she said. She patted my hand and stepped into the cold night. I folded my handouts and followed.

ONCE UPON A TIME . . .
Bernadette Adora

It was an old black 'n white photograph stuffed into a fancy silver frame that a dear girlfriend reached up and grabbed off my book shelf; she began immediately to tease me. After studying the seventeen year old girl in a full length gown with her daddy in tails proudly escorting her onto a ballroom floor, the young girl's patent-leather hair still glistening through the faded image, my friend pronounced, "Definitely, 'once upon a time when we were Colored!'" And then she threw her head back and laughed, and I shook my own head, which was cut in a short, clean-lined Afro and demanded, "Give me that back, you don't have any respect!" After which, I laughed hard myself, 'cause she was right; she was right-on!

Growing up in Detroit in the fifties and sixties was for me, a fine time to be Colored, to be Negro, to be Black, to be African-American, to be who I was and who I could and would become despite segregation; my father's hard working, hard drinking ways; our little bitty money stretched to its limits. There was a whole lotta hope and determination for so-called, better times; it was then that we could and we would nearly always envision more. Be it the new thought understanding that is prevalent today in books and on Oprah, or just because we gave it our all despite what society said we could and could not have or could and could not be -- better times did come to pass. Quite simply stated, it is my unadorned and unabashed belief that it remains a privilege to help keep the dream alive, to help keep those so-called, better times just keep on keepin' on. Period.

BRAVE RUNNER
Ellie Searl

 I lined up beside the others. I crouched, positioned my skates, and waited for the whistle.

The others came from out of town. They looked cold and uncomfortable in tight, stretch nylon suits with matching gloves and hoods. Their black lace-up skates with those extended, smooth-tipped blades looked impractical and awkward. How would they grip the ice? They'd slip and slide all over the place.

I'd been figure skating on Lake Champlain in upstate New York since I was a toddler, and by the time I was twelve, I was a marvel on ice. I could skate both forward and backward. I could make almost perfect, though wide, figure eights. I could even skate on one leg without falling down. And I liked speed. I skated faster and farther than all of my friends, so I entered the Winter Carnival Speed Skating Competition.

I didn't know it at the time, but I was way out of my league.

The whistle blew. I shoved off. The others sailed past me. Their elongated blades swooshed and clinked, spewing sprays of shaved ice. Lithe, slender bodies swayed in hypnotic rhythm. I was stunned.

So calm, so fluid, competing with each other at a pace I didn't expect. The heat of shame stung my cheeks and ears. Long legs drifted effortlessly ahead of me in seamless, congruent strides. Arms swung left, then right, then left again, in parallel formations. Wiry torsos leaned forward and a bit to the side as they banked around the track.

Hindered by thick wool snow pants, I chugged along with as much oomph as I could muster, my chunky legs trying to gain speed and make headway. I was desperate to prove I was good.

Chin leading, arms akimbo, I pushed my metal blades in an acceleration of flying frenzy. My short legs lunged faster and faster, faster and faster, bouncing on ice patches, tripping on the tips of my skates.

For each one of the racers' smooth, effortless glides, my feet made three, maybe four, awkward thrusts. The muscles in my thighs stung. My throat ached from shallow, rapid breaths of raw, frigid air. Ice shavings pitted my face and stung my eyes.

Arms flailing, heart pounding, I hurtled forward, the pain in my legs growing unbearable. Frost clung to my eyelashes; my fingers felt sticky with sweat inside my mittens. The others elegantly and effortlessly sliced through space with confident complacency - in no particular hurry, expending no particular energy.

I began sprinting wildly on my serrated tips. Dagger points formed mini-craters as the metal teeth dug into the ice. Chunks of frozen shards flew every which way.

I bounced and bolted in a state of hysterical panic. I was the Carnival Clown entertaining the crowd with idiotic gyrations and wild, toe-dancing jigs while the real race glided along in regal splendor.

Embarrassed tears clouded my vision. I wanted it over. *Just don't fall!* Finally, in a desperate lurch, I pitched headlong across the finish line and collapsed into a snow pile.

There I sprawled, limp and exhausted. I began to sob. How would I face my friends? I'd forever and always be known as Stumble-Bum-on-Ice.

A distant voice startled me. "And Third Place goes to Ellie Volckmann!"

With reclaimed dignity I stood proudly to receive my Bronze Medal at the Annual Westport Winter Carnival Speed Skating Championship.

The sheer force of my determined twelve-year-old spirit and grit had plummeted me across the finish line ahead of four out-of-town, trained racers who looked abashed and bewildered in their skinny nylon suits and silly skates.

I wore that ribbon of honor around my neck all day long and into the next week.

BIONIC-FOOTED MOM
Mary Lou Edwards

The logic behind an obese woman torturing herself in a girdle to look five pounds thinner always escaped me, but my reasoning skills totally vanished when it came to shoes. At 5'1" I counted on platforms to give me that long, lean look.

As newlyweds, we traveled to Central and South America with my shoe wardrobe consisting solely of platform espadrilles and high-heeled sandals. Not a pragmatic choice, but, of course, looking good is ever so important when crawling through ruins, and crawl I did. Had it not been for an eighty-three year old Yale professor lending me a hand as we trudged to Machu Picchu, I'd have been limping on my own.

After delivering his umpteenth "I do not understand your insistence on wearing those freaking shoes..." lecture, my 6'2" sanctimonious and sensibly shod spouse time and again left me in the dust. His admonitions only stopped when he became weak from altitude sickness (a big problem for tall people) and I transformed into the little pack mule lugging our bags through Peru and Colombia.

By the time we returned to the States I was ready for orthopedic boots, but I am a slow learner. I continued prancing in bound-feet type shoes for many more years until surgery and titanium foot rods brought my platform fetish to a halt.

I was delighted that my daughter sprouted past me as an adolescent. When she carried flip-flops to her prom "just in case," I knew I had raised a practical fashionista capable of standing on her own two feet - and in comfort to boot. She would define beauty on her own terms.

Her feet would probably never trigger airport security.

Pocketbook
Power
Prosperity

If You Don't . . .

. . . control your own money, enjoy what you have, value yourself, and recognize the difference between what's in your pocket and what's in your head, you will never have enough.

HOPEFUL
Bernadette Adora

My relationship to money is fairly simple: hopeful. Hopeful for me, for the world's poor, for every doggone body – I suppose, I'm something like the Miss America, who wishes for world peace! Growing up in the fifties in a family that was working class with decidedly middle class expectations, expectations eventually realized, may be the reason I copied my mother's more materialistic ways of living. My dad, on the other hand, had more basic needs; he appreciated the simple life.

Many expired credit cards later, as a mother of an adult daughter, I decided a few years ago that my work was done. It was time to look at the "next step," the one that would lead me toward my dreams postponed, one of which included early retirement. I chose a book to start me rolling; I was behind in planning for the future – I had a lot of catching up to do. "Finances" was a dirty eight-letter word, and I needed a little self-help, which I found in one book that for a discounted, $14.95 not including tax could boost my attitude toward the subject. The exercise I chose sent me in the following direction: every morning, I wrote myself a "pretend" check beginning with $1,000 on Day One, which increased each day by an additional thousand dollars. The only caveat - I was required to spend the entire amount within 24 hours. Further, I was required to keep a record of each daily credit and all debits. It was suggested that if the exercise was followed faithfully for one year, 66 million pretend dollars would be mine for whatever my heart desired. I made it to nearly four months.

I devised an elaborate routine for receiving and managing this miracle windfall with the aid of online shopping sites and catalogues to acquire STUFF, a whole lotta STUFF. I set out on new my prosperity mission. I became a frequent visitor of Tiffany's – for me, family, and friends; I even placed a deposit one day and picked up a not-so modest, fully equipped BMW the next. In one month, I was able to make a sizeable down payment on a houseboat on a bay clear across the country. By month two, I began maintaining a small but comfortable apartment in New York (I live in Chicago), I set-off building a pretend closet full of designer clothes, and as I noted earlier, went about acquiring lots of other STUFF!

After about six weeks, I was stuffed - stuffed up and bored. Eventually, it became a chore to spend this imaginary money each and every night, which I did at bedtime. I began staying up later and later trying to be true to the task at hand and the fun ran out – it was all gone! But being task oriented, I stayed the course. It was nearing the eighth week while in a hurry one night, I created a scholarship foundation in my mother's name for children growing up in a Detroit neighborhood she had loved dearly. It was quick and easy to do and so, I did it. A few days later, I created a second foundation, one for my daughter, who is an attorney and an advocate for juvenile justice. A week later, a third and final foundation was created, one for housing and educating the street children in Cape Town, South Africa.

Now the fun was back in the game and what fun I had building three separate and wonderful foundations. And once again, I became a stranger to Tiffany's and exclusive online shopping. I created business plans (simplified, but plans nonetheless), hired staff, purchased equipment, leased property, quit my job to manage these full-time endeavors (but remember, we are still in imaginary mode.) By the beginning of the fourth fun packed but exhausting month, I stopped. It dawned on me that I understood the exercise, which had helped change my mind-set. So what happened with my plan for tomorrow? I readjusted my thinking. I learned that when it came down to it, it was not about STUFF after all and growing old with a lifestyle that I never found comfortable, if truth be told. It was about building a life, my life more sincerely, which did not mean driving large or living large or appearing large. It was about moving the largess to my true heart's desire. I acquired a prosperity consciousness that did not resemble the one I started out imaging on Day One. After getting out of my own way, I fed my spirit easily, joyfully, and productively. Each evening, I turned to new endeavors with a hopeful and creative attitude, and it all came together for me. I began to understand my relationship to money.

It has been only a couple of years since playing at that game, yet a sense of hopefulness continues to seep into more and more of what I think and what I do. Somehow in getting out of my ancient groove and out from under purchasing … stuff … "my cup overflows" took on new meaning. It has become more about what I feel and what I create and the possibilities for new creation rather than obtaining objects. And while I might hear a collective, *Dahhh*, following this statement, don't we usually pay attention to the objects, the stuff? Now, I'm still a beauty junkie; however, acquisition is no longer a main sporting event, it is an occasional pleasure. And if my memory is correct, it is not written, "my credit card overflows and so does my closet." I think I finally got it. So for now, I remain an optimist, a woman, who sees her finances in a hopeful, positive way, one that is empowering through the use of creativity, feelings, imagination, and yes, some good old fashion sweat equity. There is more than light at the end of this tunnel; there is a bright beam leading my steps straight ahead 'cause I've learned to remain hopeful.

DOESN'T MAKE CENTS
Ellie Searl

How about a free will offering?

Eloise never quite understood the concept of a positive cash flow.

There is something about asking for money that knots my stomach. I get nervous and sweaty just thinking about it. I'd never make it as a prostitute. I wouldn't earn enough cash to buy the outfit and overhead necessary for success when cavorting with scum: slinky clothes, stiletto heels, cigarettes, crack cocaine, alcohol, and a rat-infested tenement in the slums. Not only would I charge too little for the humiliation of performing demeaning acts with creeps, I'd have to give more than half of my meager take to some pimp, who would most likely beat me up for being a useless earner.

It disturbs me that I'm too shy, or more likely, too insecure to charge for my services. Am I not "good enough"? Is my product not up to the standards of the general public? What am I afraid will happen if I charge too much? Or too little?

I'm a self-taught graphic designer. I design brochures, booklets, all-occasion greeting cards, posters, photograph collages, and other projects. But I'm a terrible judge of my own work. Others have said, "Ellie, this is so creative. It's so beautiful. It must have taken a pile of time! How do you come up with such clever ideas?"

"I don't know; it just happens." Fortunately I have enough self-respect to keep the ah-shucks reply completely unassuming, *not* accompanied by batting eyelashes and a receding body slump.

This is not to say I don't like to get paid for my services. I like to get paid - a lot! I just don't like to charge. Like most insecure people, I want my product to be loved and wanted so much by my clients they will set the price higher than I would ever set for myself.

I want an exchange like this:

> *"This is way too much; please, just give me half of that!"*
> *"Oh, no, Ellie, I'll give you even more! You're so worth it!"*

That's how to get paid in a perfect world.

When Kathy flipped through the pages of my most recent creation, *"A Year of Celebration,"* a calendar gift book she had commissioned me to make for her friend's birthday, she exclaimed about its beauty, its creativity, and the obvious pile of time it took.

"So, how much do I owe you?" Kathy took out her checkbook.

This is when the 'what-am-I-worth?' ache grabs me in the gut.

It's underhanded, I know, but blatant manipulation is a good way to monitor someone's appraisal barometer. I maneuver opinions out of people in order to discover what they *really* think of my work. If they say "ok" to giving me a free-will offering, that means they're not crazy about the product, and the initial excited flattery was really just 'hide-the-disappointment-in-niceties to make her feel good.' That tells me to back off. But if they insist on a giving me *more* money than a paltry contribution, well, then maybe, just maybe, I actually made a product they like . . . and want to buy.

"Just give me what you want to. I had fun making it." I wait for Kathy to respond.

"No way! Look what you've done here. There are 26 color pages, you've included each month of the year, you've cloned our faces into just about every picture, and you've used tons of ink. It's wonderful, and I'm going to pay you royally for this fabulous book."

The most I've ever set as an actual fee for any project was for the cost of the paper. I've never charged for the price of ink, the time spent working, wear and tear on my computer and printer, the electricity, any traveling involved, not to mention the wine, cheese, gin martinis with olives, coffee, and Alka Seltzer that kept me sustained at the computer until 2:00 am while numbing my butt or freezing my fingers because the heat was turned down to 55 degrees five hours earlier.

Once, I didn't charge anything. I brought a friend into my home, helped her design thank you cards using my computer, and then printed all 60 cards with my card stock paper on my color printer while we drank a nice Merlot. She wanted to pay me, but I lied and told her I do this all the time . . . for the love of it. I know; I'm an idiot. Did I mention it was my Merlot?

I tell Kathy, "Ok, How about $50.00?"

"How about I triple that. You can't do work like this and not get paid what it's worth! You're cheating yourself!" Kathy was adamant.

The manipulation paid off this time, probably because she was a friend of mine. The next person will have to be just as good exploitation material if I am to make any kind of living selling my free-lance graphic design projects - or anything else, for that matter. If I do decide to try the oldest profession, I'd at least have the basic inventory readily available.

ALWAYS HAVE A PLAN
Mary Lou Edwards

"Park your car, Doc! Right here, Doc! Park your car, Doc!"

Those sing-song words meant the White Sox were at Comiskey and my brother and his buddies were making money.

Never being included in the action bothered me so I went to tattle-tale to my dad. I found him tuned to his transistor radio.

"Dad," I asked, "Anthony gets an allowance like me so why is he parking cars for money?"

"It's always better to make your own money," he answered, "then you can be independent and take care of yourself."

The seed was planted.

"When I get bigger, I'm going to park cars and make money to take care of you and Mom," I promised.

"Girls can't park cars," he said, just as Bob Elson announced strike three. But the Sox were winning and he wasn't ticked off so he didn't shoo me away. "It's harder for women to make money because there are a lot of jobs they can't do."

"So that means I get an allowance forever?"

"No, it means someday you'll marry a man who'll take care of you and you'll get a good education just in case something happens to him."

"What if I can't find a man who wants me," I worried, thinking of Angelina down the street who never married.

"Well, you'll have your education to fall back on so you can be independent and take care of yourself. Go play with your sister. The Sox are up to bat," he said, as he turned his attention back to the game.

Did he just say, I wondered, that I could only be independent if something happened to my husband or if I didn't get married? If you were someone's wife, you couldn't be independent? But what if a woman's husband said she could be independent?

I had more questions, but I knew better than to keep bugging Dad when he was listening to baseball. Why couldn't girls park cars? Why were the boys telling men where to park—they didn't own the street. Why did so many doctors go to the ballgame?

There was no asking my brother. He'd tell me to quit sticking my nose where it didn't belong. Besides, even though boys thought they knew it all, they really didn't. He probably wouldn't know why it was harder for women to make money or how I could find a rich man to take care of me.

Luckily I had a good brain. Even my brother said I was smart for a girl. I'd figure this out for myself plus get an education just in case no man wanted to marry me. And if no one wanted to marry me, that wouldn't be so terrible; boys didn't impress me. I mean, God didn't even trust them to have babies. If I stayed on the honor roll, maybe I could even skip the marriage part and jump right in to taking care of myself.

True, Dad handed over his paycheck to Mom every Friday but was it really hers? She didn't go to work every day and earn it.

I almost never saw her buy anything for herself. Did she figure she was lucky not to have a job so she was happy to stay home and just cook, clean, mop, sew, bake, grocery shop, wash windows, iron, do laundry, scrub floors, take care of us kids, drag around the Electro-Lux and drink coffee? Was she glad she didn't drive and that Daddy took her everywhere it was too far to walk?

She was dependent with a capital D. For years she'd wanted to move out of the old neighborhood. She'd say, "Jim, let's buy a house." But he'd always say, "Mary, now is not the time. We've got three kids to put through college." Couldn't they vote on some things? But voting probably wouldn't make any difference because it would be a tie and Dad was always the tie-breaker. Sometimes she could say what she thought but she really couldn't change anything. He was the boss.

Long before I'd heard the perverse version of the Golden Rule, "He who has the gold, rules." I figured dependency was not a good thing so I just watched how it all worked and finally decided that I'd have to make my own rules. One day after school I made my list based on things my Mom did or didn't do and which I thought would make a difference.

RULES FOR INDEPENDENCE
1. Make a plan.
2. Go to college.
3. Drive a car.
4. Get a good job.
5. Save my money.
6. Dye my hair.
7. Smoke cigarettes and wear lipstick.
8. Don't listen to men.
9. Don't let a husband boss me around.
10. Make my own decisions.

I found my Mother in the kitchen slaving over the ironing board.

"Mom," I asked, "could you read these and tell me what you think? I made some rules so I can be independent when I grow up."

She put the iron on its little metal resting plate, picked up my notebook and began reading. Her first "hmmm . . . ." sounded like she was thinking "OK, not bad," but her next "hmmm . . .", as she neared the bottom of the page, sounded like "Really now? Is that so?"

She was quiet for a minute as she placed my notes on the table and retrieved her still hot iron. Finally she gave me one of those what-am-I-going-to-do-with-you smiles, and said, "What you wrote is very interesting. In fact, the first five ideas are excellent, but I thought you hated rules."

"Mom, I don't hate all rules," I informed her, "just stupid rules, like only taking ten books out of the library at one time. These rules are different. They're my rules. They're for when I grow up."

"So you decide which rules are stupid and which are important?" she probed.

"Yes, didn't you read number ten?" I responded in a voice like Sister Mary Perpetua, my teacher. " I'll make my own decisions. I decide if something is stupid. I'll use my own brain to decide if something is important," I ranted, wanting to add, "And I already decided that ironing is a waste of time," but I bit my tongue. Instead I continued, "Number nine says no husband will boss me around. Did you read the rules carefully, Momma?"

She probably was thinking, "Oh, God, this girl is never going to get married. She'll be way too much trouble," but instead she said, "Well, Honey, going to college, getting a good job and saving money should help you take charge of your own life, but why on earth would you want to smoke cigarettes and dye your hair?"

44

I didn't want to tell her that Red-Headed Ann, a glamorous woman who lived on the next block, smoked Viceroys, dyed her hair (my girlfriend Donna said you could tell because it was almost orange) and drove a convertible, always looked like she was having a good time. I didn't want to confess that, not only did I plan to be independent, but glamorous as well. I just knew Red-Headed Ann would never waste a minute ironing sheets and pillowcases.

As if reading my mind, Momma said, while maneuvering the hot metal point of the iron into the corner of my father's shirt collar, "You probably think smoking and dyed hair are glamorous. Well, let me tell you smoking is bad for your lungs and dyeing your hair is expensive and turns your hair into straw so you'd better find out what you're getting into first." Then holding the iron down on the shirt for so long I thought she was going to scorch it, she added, "You have a lot to learn, Missy."

I thought she might be getting irritated with me, and then I was sure of it when she gave me a fake smile and said, "Just wait and see what happens when you fall in love and get married, Miss Smarty Pants."

I knew by the way she smirked "Miss Smarty Pants" she was telling me there were things I was too young to understand and that even with a plan, life doesn't always go your way.

I wondered if she'd had a plan that changed when she got married. I wanted to ask, but I thought she might feel bad if that was what had happened. The thought of that made me very sad, so I kept my mouth shut. Instead I said, "You're the world's best Mother! I love you so much. I just wish you had time for a little fun."

In my head, though, I said, "It's going to be different for me, Momma. You just wait and see."

WHAT I FOUND IN THE BARGAIN BIN
Carolyn B Healy

When I was growing up, a great day out for my mother and me was a trip east down 111th Street from our apartment in Morgan Park, past the high school, two neighborhoods over to Roseland, home of Gately's Peoples' Store. Gately's was kind of a combo department store and discount store before there was such a thing.

The southernmost neighborhood in Chicago, Morgan Park was a leafy hilly place, site of a private school with a handsome campus, and of a limestone library that we could see from our second floor apartment. Roseland was plainer, with its modest houses and tidy lawns set in a firm grid, the home of our rival high school. But it was one of our favorite haunts, thanks to Gately's.

There was nothing fancy about the store. I remember squeaky wooden floors and glass-topped counters, and a giant center staircase. It had all the typical departments – ladies' dresses, hosiery, fabrics and notions, children's clothes. There was even a crowded lunch counter with tall skinny stools, I think in the basement, where you could grab a Coke if your shopping wore you out.

We'd look for whatever was the excuse for the trip – a dress for a special occasion, play clothes, a pattern and fabric that would make it to the living room closet but probably not into production. We always had more ambition than follow-through.

The best part was located in the center of the first floor – the bargain bins piled high with turtlenecks, mittens, sweaters, blouses, pajamas, socks. We'd leave with a dark green bag with Gately's written in yellow script, as satisfied as hunters dragging home their prey.

On the way home, we'd stop for dinner at White Castle on 111th just west of the store. Nestled next to the multi-story YMCA, it had an Edward Hopper "Nighthawks" quality. We'd order sliders, those mini-burgers steamed and covered with onions, each tucked into its own cardboard box, and then for dessert, lemon meringue pie. As we ate, we'd rate our bargains, reliving their pleasures as golfers do the great putt on 14.

Money was not a big issue then in my life, just a means to ends like turtlenecks, food, fun, something to spend as little as possible of but not to worry about. I know now that my single mother was doing the worrying while successfully hiding it from me.

Since then, I've had my run-ins with money – the bounced checks for my $5 a week expenses once I went away to college without a clue about how to balance a checkbook, for instance. And much later the midnight anxiety about how on earth I was going to make payroll when I had my own business and my customers didn't pay me on time, or at all.

But my modest start did me a favor – my financial set point is firmly and permanently fixed nice and low. I definitely love bargains more than I love spending. Nowadays, on the rare occasion that I overdo it on one big purchase or a flurry of smaller ones and take myself over my long-established threshold, I'll be sorry. Even though I can afford the splurge now, I feel a little sick and a little guilty, as if I had eaten the whole lemon meringue pie myself.

I've transferred my allegiance now to consignment shops and outlet malls, but the thrill of those outings with Mom is long gone. I'd give a lot to wander back through Gately's aisles for an afternoon with her and see how much of what I remember was actually there.

Do other people have Gately's memories too? Apparently they do if my discovery of www.gatelysstoreinroseland.blogspot.com is any indication. The next time I get an impulse to shop, I think I'll explore there instead. Think of the money I'll save.

Savor the Memories

There Are cooks . . .

. . . who swear by James Beard. There are cooks who pull out scribbled notes from Mom when a culinary masterpiece is required. There are those who allow the season to dictate the ingredients for a memorable dish and still others who fly by the seat of their pants using ingredients on hand. No matter how one goes about creating a meal, the one thing we know for sure is that long after the last crumb has been consumed, memories will remain.

MEATBALLS ON BITTERBRUSH
Ellie Searl

It's remarkable what an aroma can do. Just a whiff of Italian cooking takes my thoughts across the country to a little spot of heaven and a life-changing adventure in the Pacific Northwest.

My journey started at the curb of Seattle's United Departures where Dick and Carol handed me the keys.

"Call us if you have trouble. Don't forget - you'll be out of cell range and radio reception once you start up the pass. The instructions for SIRIUS are in the glove compartment. Have fun on your adventure, Kiddo. The kerosene lamp is always full. Help yourself to the rum in the freezer. Do you remember where the generator is? . . . Watch out for the deer . . .and the hunters. Wear red."

The groceries purchased at a little IGA rattled around as I drove toward the mountains. I should have packed better, but I was in a hurry to catch the last sharp images of the waning October afternoon. Bottles collided with each other and against my suitcases. The pungent odor of deli peppers and dill pickles filled the car; I hoped sloshed drippings weren't saturating the carpet.

I meandered up the winding roads on the west side of North Cascades Highway toward Washington Pass. Autumn splendor dotted the landscape with copper and rust. Shafts of sunlight streamed through splits in the valleys. I stopped at look-out points to photograph breathtaking golden panoramas. The intense clarity of the late October afternoon made this one-woman-adventure-into-the-wilderness exciting and celebratory.

I was on my way to house-sit Dick and Carol's isolated cabin in the forest while they sailed in the Caribbean. Their Golden Retriever, River, had been placed in a kennel, so I wouldn't be required to dog-sit as well. A few years ago, I agreed to dog-sit for my other brother, and after that, dog-sitting was about as appealing to me as swimming in oatmeal. Even though there would be one dog, not two as before, and even though River wasn't deaf and blind, didn't ooze puss from his eyes, didn't need eye drops, didn't take four varieties of pills wrapped in bread - or stuck in peanut butter - or mushed into soggy dog food, and didn't chase around the pool yelping at swimmers,
I still refused. I did, however, agree to take care of the cat, Cricket, despite the fact that she was deteriorating from old age and a failing kidney. I knew that Cricket was afraid of people and wouldn't show her face until I had moved around the cabin for at least four days. And cats, sick or not, take care of themselves – as long as they can locate their food, water, and litter box. She was my kind of companion.

I took too much time admiring the changing colors of fading daylight. When the sun finally slid behind the stillness of Lake Diablo, dusk, combined with looming mountain shadows, made driving menacing. The lack of guardrails at outcroppings floating over vertical drop-offs swept away the casual security I had felt just a few hours earlier. I was nervous. The smell of onions, garlic, and pickle juice was strong and nauseating. By the time I crested Washington Pass and started down the steep-graded s-curves, it was pitch dark. My SUV veered around twists in the highway just a few feet from precipitous ledges that hovered over sharp drops to the valley floor.

I rounded the bend where, according to my brother, some kids careened to their death because they weren't paying attention. As excited as I had been by the exquisite views a few hours before, I couldn't look. I clutched the wheel and kept my eyes on the road. Headlights beamed on red and brown where green should have been. The dull colors were out of sync with postcard prettiness. A sense of doom magnified my already waning excitement, and I worried that global warming and infectious diseases were destroying the forests of the Pacific Northwest. I began thinking that my venture into the unknown was not such a bright idea. Perhaps I shouldn't have left the company and comfort of my husband and home in Chicago to sail out on my own to this god-forsaken, desolate place. Not even the trees knew how to stay alive.

After convincing myself that those unfortunate dead kids were brainless blockheads on a drunken binge, I navigated the curves with invented courage - easing and braking, easing and braking - down the east side of the mountain, along the river, and then finally, up a steep rise to the safety of the cabin on Bitterbrush Road.

The night was eerily quiet, except for the stones crunching under my feet and a slight swish of branches high over head. Ebony stillness surrounded me. A symphony of stars in sparkling constellations I couldn't name shone on me with mysterious silent glory from an inky sky. Gentle breezes nudged pine needles and oak leaves into singing their tree-songs. Cool air carried the scents of spruce and cedar.

I entered the warmth of the cabin and the joy of my brother's life with Carol. I found a welcome note and house instructions beside a red and white striped bowl filled with Bombay Sapphire Gin, Martini and Rossi Dry Vermouth, a jar of olives, and a cut-crystal cocktail glass. The greeting was sweet and gracious. I placed the martini makings on the painted pine hutch next to the already-flowering Christmas cactus. Night magnificence, forest calm, and cabin lamplight revitalized me after that long, unnerving drive over Washington Pass in the dark. I opened a bottle of Champagne, drank a toast to my journey, and with glass in hand, searched for Cricket among the nooks, crannies, and quilts of her home.

In the next three weeks, I would go to the farmers market in Twisp and buy sunflowers and home-made, orchard-fresh peach pie from the 85-year-old woman who baked it, pastries from the Cinnamon Twisp Bakery, and double-churned ice cream from Sheri's Sweet Shoppe. I would visit the Winthrop Art Gallery and watch glass being sculpted into vases and bowls. I would drive along the Columbia River and marvel at the immensity and grandeur of our world, and with a packed lunch, take a four-hour sight-seeing boat trip up glacial Lake Chelan to Stehekin outpost. I would sit on the back porch in the rain and work on the New York Times Sunday crossword puzzle, and watch humming birds quiver around the feeders when the sun came out. I would find a Washington Mutual Bank in Omak, 40 miles away, and get my nails done on the same trip. I would congratulate myself on not reaching a state of panic when I woke up at 2:00 am and thought I was blind because it was so dark that it didn't matter if my eyes were open or closed. And then I would scramble for a flashlight in pitch black terror and phone the electric company to ask if there had been a power outage.

I would stroke Cricket, who found me sooner than four days after my arrival, and who sat on my lap and purred despite her fear of humans. I would tend Cricket as her health declined and sadly caress her on her final days and feel her soak up all the love I could give her in her last home under the majesty of the Cascade Mountains. I would take her to the vet and stand beside her and hold her as the difficult but necessary decisions were made to relieve her of her pain and misery. Then I would drive back to the cabin with an empty cat crate knowing that Carol's buddy of 17 years would not be there when she returned home to sneak up on her and snuggle again.

I would read books, write in my journal, drive through the forest, walk along the river, drink champagne, sleep when I felt like it, and wear red. I would create savory meals while sipping martinis or white wine bottled in Wenatchee. I'd make fresh vegetable soup and seared ahi tuna with asparagus and BLT's with fake bacon and turkey cheeseburgers with lots of ketchup. And I'd make an abundance of scrumptious baked Italian meatballs, so many meatballs that I'd eat them again and again with spaghetti or as hot sandwiches or just plain cold, straight out of the refrigerator.

I would stand on the mountainside and look down along the green and orange vastness of the Methow River Valley and thank my lucky stars that I had this opportunity to live here by myself for a short, beautiful time. And I would forever treasure these moments of my journey into self-hood, self-discovery, self-sufficiency, and self-appreciation.

When my senses detect even a hint of oregano or basil, this memory wafts over me and takes me to that little cabin on Bitterbrush where I rejuvenated my soul.

BAKED ITALIAN MEATBALLS

❖1 onion, chopped
❖1 green pepper, chopped
❖2 – 3 Tbsp Olive oil
❖1 slice bread, soaked in milk
❖1 pound ground turkey or beef
❖1 egg

❖1 can Italian stewed tomatoes
❖¼ cup Ketchup
❖1 large jar marinara (or favorite spaghetti sauce)
❖Salt and pepper (to taste)
❖Parmesan cheese (to taste)

Preheat oven to 250°. Sauté chopped onion and pepper in olive oil until soft; let cool a little. Combine stewed tomatoes, Ketchup, and marinara into a sauce. Mash the tomatoes if too chunky.

Mix together sautéed onion and pepper, milk-soaked bread, egg, ground meat, and about ½ to ¾ cup of the sauce mixture. Add salt and pepper as desired. Mixture will be sloppy. Shape mixture into meatballs.

Spread some sauce in bottom of lightly greased baking pan, and place meatballs on sauce in one layer. Add a little more sauce, but don't completely cover the meatballs. Sprinkle with parmesan cheese. Bake at 250° for 1½ hours.

THE TORTURE HOUR
Mary Lou Edwards

 The dinner hour started in its usual manner with warnings of don't touch, it's hot, be careful. Mom placed a Pyrex platter on the table guaranteed to jump start every salivary gland on the planet. Wisps of steam rose from the bubbly gravy and stringy mozzarella smothered yet another culinary masterpiece. It was hard to believe that such an auspicious beginning, replete with the heavenly aroma of basil and olive oil, could turn into a meal from hell, but we'd been through the drill often enough to know the inevitable conclusion.

The minute my father opened the cedar-lined closet doors the drama began. Just hearing the creaky wheels of the cart that held the behemoth Magnavox reel-to-reel tape recorder roll over the slick wood floor would be enough to start the nervous snickers and stage whispers to mom.

"Please, Mom," my brother begged, "don't let him ruin our dinner again."

"You know you hate it too," I'd hiss. "Be honest, Mom, and make him stop."

"I'm not hungry anymore," my sister would whine.

"You kids had better be quiet," Mom would warn, giving us a take-no-prisoners look. "Don't make trouble and get him angry!"

By then Dad had threaded the huge circular wheels with the magic music recently captured on magnetic tape and was taking his seat at the head of the table. As we bowed our heads for the requisite murmuring "Bless us, O Lord, for these Thy gifts..." we knew the amen would signal the beginning of the torture hour also known as the music appreciation lesson. In reality, it was the precursor to waterboarding.

Even the heaping plates of fabulous food could not anesthetize us from the musical cacophony that was to ensue.

With the loud click of the PLAY button, the air was filled with Lawrence Welk leading his band of acoustic terrorists with "Ana one, ana two, ana three..." in a nauseating version of the Beer Barrel Polka or his Champagne Lady of Music warbling "I'm Forever Blowing Bubbles."

By the end of the first stanza, the deterioration of the family dinner had begun.

With each grating, offensive squeak of the string assassins, my brother would grimace and clutch his heart as though being attacked, my sister would knock over a glass of milk hoping to get sent to her room, our dog Skipper would skitter off suddenly remembering a prior engagement and my martyr mother would be looking heavenward as though begging God to strike her deaf immediately. My father's steely-eyed glares of disgust at this contemptible conduct elicited more wisecracks and uncontrollable laughter inevitably resulting in the family sin worthy of capital punishment—milk-pouring-from-someone's-nose-who-was-acting-silly!

"It is sinful to waste milk and revolting," Dad would intone and, at this point, the simple dysfunctional family dinner would turn into an event guaranteed to provide full-blown post-traumatic stress disorder.

Snapping the STOP button, he would launch into tirades about rudeness, ingratitude and stupidity interspersed with "You kids don't know good music." His tongue lashing about our being unteachable was rather paradoxical since it was Mr. Welk who would declare, "Myron and I will now do a solo together." After all, we'd know the difference between the Roman numeral I and a capital I on a cue card and wouldn't announce, "And now for a song from World War Eye." But we were the idiots? The irony was knee deep but totally wasted on my dad who'd pontificate, "They don't write songs like this anymore . . . ." as "Mairzy doats and dozy doats and liddle lamzy divey…" blared in the background.

Actually my father's harangues were more palatable than Welk's prototype elevator muzak. Somehow our digestive tracts had become accustomed to my dad's force feedings of ridicule and shame, but our lower GI's never quite adjusted to the diabetic inducing renditions of "Somewhere Over the Rainbow."

MARY SCALISE'S EGGPLANT PARMIGIANA

- Olive oil for frying
- 1 large eggplant
- Flower for dredging
- 2 eggs, beaten
- 1 quart Italian tomato sauce
- 1 pound fresh mozzarella, sliced
- 1 pound grated imported Romano or Parmesan cheese
- Italian spices to taste: basil, parsley, fennel seed, oregano
- Salt and pepper

Preheat the oven to 375°. Peel the eggplant, and slice crossways into ¼-inch thick rounds. Dredge the eggplant slices in flour and dip into the eggs, shaking off any excess. Fry slices in hot oil until golden, about two minutes on each side. Remove from oil and drain on paper towels.

Cover the bottom of a baking dish with a layer of fried eggplant and spread some Italian sauce on top. Cover eggplant with slices of mozzarella, and sprinkle with Romano or Parmesan cheese and Italian spices. Add salt and pepper to taste. Repeat the layering until all ingredients are used, finishing with a layer of mozzarella. Bake for ½ hour, or until cheese is melted and golden.

WRITING THE BOOK ON PICKY EATERS
Carolyn B Healy

Some people remember certain classics from their childhood bookshelves – *Black Beauty*, *Green Eggs and Ham*, *The Velveteen Rabbit*. For me, it's the little-known *Cheese, Peas and Chocolate Pudding* by Betty Van Witsen, last published in 1971. It tells the story of a little boy who would eat only those three foods and nothing else. Thanks to my mother I heard it hundreds of times. When I get hooked on something, I stay hooked. At least I was until I joined the *Weekly Reader* Book Club and got started on *The Pink Motel*, *No Children No Pets*, *Leader Dog* and the like. And then Nancy Drew came into my life and I put childhood things aside.

By the time I needed it again, *Cheese, Peas and Chocolate Pudding* was long gone, out of print and available only in my memory. One miraculous afternoon in a pediatrician's office, I found a copy in a stack of tattered children's books. I persuaded the receptionist to let me take it home overnight to copy.

Unlike *Catcher in the Rye* and *Dick and Jane*, which I have re-read with disappointment, *C,P and CP* held up over time. (SPOILER ALERT: there are currently no copies available on amazon.com, but just in case you experience a serendipitous discovery like mine and get to read the book on your own, you may not want to read the rest of this paragraph.) It had tension – earnest parents try to get him to eat. It had drama – he sits under the dining table refusing dinner. It had climax and resolution – a scrap of his older brother's hamburger drops into his mouth and he finds it delicious. And it had realism – after that, he only eats cheese, peas, chocolate pudding and hamburger.

In a twist that suggests that the universe has a sense of humor, I gave birth to that little boy in real life, in the person of my daughter Katy. While gobbling her way through boxes of rice cereal and jar after jar of baby sweet potatoes, she spit out all meat products and anything green. As a toddler, she graduated to a monochromatic diet of grilled cheese, macaroni and cheese and applesauce. No candy, no cookies, no meat, no frills. I could have written a book. If the term picky eater didn't already exist, I would have had to coin it.

It wasn't that she didn't experiment some. She liked fish sticks until she found out that they were made of fish; same with tuna salad. She was briefly willing to try hot dogs as long as they touched nothing else on her plate, until someone (I suspect her older brother) told her they contain things like rat lips and cat brains. And she was the only child in America who hated chocolate.

Just like the book, her story has a happy but realistic ending, as she finally ventured out into Grandma's Cheesy Potatoes, cheese pizza and the other Grandma's mashed potatoes and eventually, the occasional pasta and chicken breast. While the color palette remained the same, she could enjoy much more variety.

Once, well into adulthood, that same brother took both of us to an Ethiopian restaurant in his neighborhood. She tried to like it but her revulsion was real and at the end of the meal, she went straight across the street for the biggest slice of pizza I've ever seen.

I have a copy of *Cheese, Peas and Chocolate Pudding* set aside for her once she gets as far as parenting. I know she will bring special insight to its reading. In honor of her, here is one of her breakthroughs, Grandma's Cheesy Potatoes.

CHEESY POTATOES

❖4 large potatoes
❖3/4 to 1 C. half and half
❖2/3 to 1 C. shredded cheese, cheddar or gruyere
❖Salt & pepper

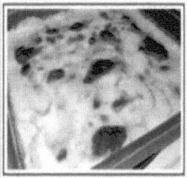

Preheat oven to 400°. Peel and thinly slice potatoes. Lightly grease a 9 x 9 glass baking dish. Place a layer of potato slices. Sprinkle with salt, pepper, and cheese. Repeat layering and end with a generous layer of cheese on top. Pour half and half over the potatoes.

Cover with foil. Bake 45 minutes. If potatoes are not yet tender, bake ten more minutes. If all the liquid is absorbed, add more half and half. Once potatoes are tender, uncover and bake 10 minutes more until cheese bubbles and browns. Wait 10 minutes before serving. Can add freshly ground nutmeg if feeding to non-picky eaters.

SWEET POTATO PIE
Bernadette Adora

When I was young, sugar was the medicine that helped soothe the soul, sugar along with savory flavors that tickled the senses and brought about a huge smile on the faces of young and old alike. Savory flavors, sugary goodness plus Rhythm and Blues -- and to be perfectly honest, put all together, it remains a soul soother. But unlike today, sugar was a weekend or holiday treat that took the form of homemade cake: double chocolate, yellow coconut, or maybe a light-as-air pound cake with a big scoop of fresh sugared strawberries on the side. Sometimes, it was a pie not long from the oven: savory sweet potato; lemon meringue; or even warm, spicy apples surrounded and protected by a perfected flaky crust. A double crust fruit cobbler was wonderful too, especially peach, but I couldn't get with cobblers made with berries -- a personal thing I suppose. But I have fond memories too of a dented metal pan brimming over with banana pudding, a large glass bowl of creamy rice pudding with more raisins than one would considered reasonable, and a modest size tub of a favorite summertime treat: vanilla ice cream cranked by hand – mercy! A small but important note here: Unlike a little sweet treat or two in a chipped dish from time to time, R&B was everyday, if not all day.

My daddy loved my mother's cooking! I honestly think that if my mother had not been gifted in the kitchen, she would have died a spinster – or maybe married some sour face man with no need or appreciation for the smells and flavors that wafted from a kitchen on Sunday afternoons after church – sometimes on

Saturdays too depending on family plans. Baked ham covered in cloves with huge round, sweet pineapple slices; pork chops smothered in gravy; lamb roast lined from top to bottom with slivers of fresh garlic and homemade mint jelly atop the stove waiting to finish; fried chicken, crispy from an egg batter dip, rolled in flour, and then seasoned just right; rabbit stew simmering in sweet-red wine sauce with spices that defied the imagination; catfish, whitefish, perch, or trout fried up in an old black, well worn, cast iron pan – daddy fished throughout the summer on the Michigan lakes and rivers; he caught our fish and brought them home, enough oft times to share with the neighbors. He lugged a pail, sometimes two, of ice filled with fish into the back door late night around bedtime, him smelling a little of Pabst Blue Ribbon Beer and pleased to be home to take hold of his wife, who didn't have time; she busying herself for our Sunday feast and shooing him away - most times. Then there were the jellies, jams, peaches, pickles, corn, to name a few, that were canned -- fruit and vegetables prepared by the bushel full from late summer to early autumn. Collard greens and mustard greens seasoned to perfection served with Louisiana Hot Sauce, never Tabasco, go figure; fried and cream corn fresh from the cob before finding a way to the pan; green beans with baby white potatoes along with bits of sugared ham; warm, light biscuits; corn bread piping hot; and not to forget the sauces and gravies for barbecues and roasts and nearly anything hot from the oven. Yup! My daddy loved my mother's cooking – those few Saturday nights and those regular, can-depend-on Sunday afternoons right after church!!!

The problem for me, the only child in a household with a way-older brother off and living his life with a beautiful, young wife, is that I was often times in the way. I was a reader and a dreamer; the kitchen was the place that I spent evenings washing up and sweeping the floor; Saturday mornings on my hands and knees with a rag, a hot bucket of water, and Mr. Clean. My mother, bless her heart, was a nervous woman much of the time, and it was easier to delegate cleaning to me and do the cooking herself. Besides, there would be plenty of time to pass along the recipes and family secrets and sleight of hand famous for making her dishes a delight. But that time never came, my daughter did reap the benefit of some lessons and a bit of craft, but by then, daddy had passed, mother retired, and I was grown -- time was too precious. Thank goodness for an early marriage to a man whose mother never cooked, if she didn't have to – that man was so grateful for everything I attempted in those early months that eventually I learned from the school of trial and error. I should go looking for that man, long moved on and out, just to thank him for his patience and optimism. I learned to cook thanks in part to his encouragement and appreciation – ahh, too bad that's all I can recommend there. But then, that, as they say, is another story.

Today, I have tucked away a few of my mother's precious recipes and special touches. It is with loving pleasure I share: Sweet Potato Pie. Since my daddy had a serious sweet-tooth, my mother kicked up the sweetness of that pie quite a bit. Most people keep the sugar reduced, especially in this new day and age, so I leave it to you. Here is a recipe, lighten up on the sugar if you wish and cheat on the crust if you must, but remember, my mother made all her pie crusts from scratch and that is what I'm including. Her pie crusts were her pride and joy. To my mother, a perfect flaky pie crust separated the woman from the girl.

FLAKY PIE CRUST

- ❖1 cup sifted flour
- ❖1/2 tsp salt
- ❖1/3 cup shortening (Crisco)
- ❖2 to 3 tablespoons of ice water

Add shortening to sifted flour and salt. Thoroughly cut in shortening. Sprinkle ice water over flour mixture and toss until it begins to hold together. Roll out the dough, place into pie pan, and trim the edge.

If time allows, make your crust ahead of time and freeze until ready to use.

Remember: For a flaky crust, barely handle the dough.

Enjoy! Now don't forget to switch on a little Rhythm and Blues to go along with this simple but sweet delight, both in the preparation and in the eatin'. Feel free to move about and swing a bit to the beat should the spirit move you; it is without question, the right accompaniment.

SWEET POTATO PIE

(Ingredients)

❖ 4 Medium or 3 large sweet potatoes, peeled (approximately 4 cups when strained* and mashed)
❖ 1 Cup dark brown sugar, packed (keep an extra ½ cup aside for the taste test below)
❖ 3 Large eggs – beat well in separate small bowl (hint: crack your eggs, one by one in a separate tiny bowl just in case one is "bad" so not to ruin the rest – an Elizabeth trick.)
❖ 1 Stick soft unsalted butter
❖ 1 Tsp vanilla extract (the best quality your budget will allow)
❖ 1 Cup half and half – or if you dare: heavy cream
❖ ½ Tsp each nutmeg and cloves**
❖ 2 Dashes salt

*My mother hated the stringiness of sweet potatoes -- she strained them through a medium sized meshed wire colander to help remove the "strings."

* * Another thing: My mother didn't believe in combining nutmeg with cinnamon in most recipes -- she was a nutmeg lady. Sometimes I cheat and add ¼ teaspoon of cinnamon -- please don't tell on me. Some folks add allspice; I never, ever saw this spice in my mother's kitchen.

SWEET POTATO PIE

(Directions)

Preheat oven to 400°. Boil or bake sweet potatoes until tender. Cool a little, but it helps if the potatoes are still warm. Beat the eggs. Whip the butter 'til creamy. Beat the warm sweet potatoes well. Add the creamy butter and the sugar to the sweet potatoes. Beat. Add the cream. Beat. Add the spices. Beat.

Taste. Think. Taste again. Adjust by adding more sugar or spices. Remember – the eggs have not been yet added.

Finally, add the eggs. Beat.

Add the mixture to a cold (frozen) pie crust that has been "fitted" to the pie pan, crimped around the edges, preferably.
(See Flaky Pie Crust Recipe)

Place in preheated oven and after about 10 minutes, lower heat to about 350°. Bake approximately one hour, but check after 45 minutes by inserting a sharp knife or wooden toothpick into the center, which should come out "clean." If too moist and mixture clings to the instrument used to check, bake for another 10-12 minutes and check again. Cool for 30 minutes before serving.

The Art of
Asking

It Starts . . .

     . . . with a question. And after that all bets are off.

> *What do you want?*
> *Do you love me?*
> *How much was that?*
> *Where have you been?*
> *Why did you say that?*
> *Do I look fat in this?*

For some, there are answers.

Elephants in Limbo
Mary Lou Edwards

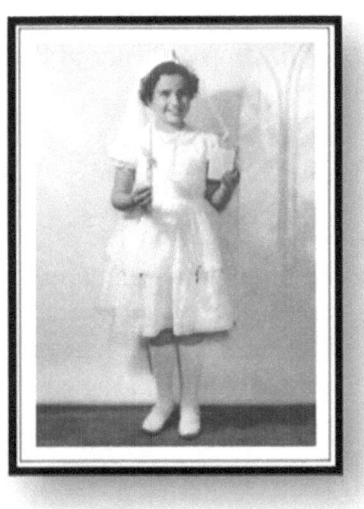

Long before learning to read books, I learned to read people. Having a father with a mercurial temperament was the catalyst, no doubt. Being on hyper-alert for glaring eyes, exasperated sighs, raised voices—the phonics of dysfunction—often, but not always, kept one out of harm's way.

A subskill necessary for people-reading fluency was learning not to ask questions. Way before 'Don't Ask, Don't Tell' became a part of America's political lexicon, I'd been trained in 'Don't You Dare Ask'—a skill I so perfected a mere raised eyebrow, a simple sideward glance was enough to STOP. RIGHT. THERE.

The list of verboten topics was endless, encompassing everything from family history to current events. Further complicating the problem was the fact that no map existed showing where the land mines lay and an innocuous inquiry often detonated an explosion of confusion that neither education nor therapy could heal.

"Dad," I asked as I knelt at the family plot in Mt. Carmel Cemetery, "why is Little Nonna and everyone buried here while Grandpa is all by himself at Oak Ridge which isn't even Catholic?"

"You're supposed to be praying for the dead not asking nosy questions that are none of your business," he said in his usual you-are-such-a-pain-in-the-neck voice as he tried to shimmy the old gravestone the years had pushed off center.

"Mom, why doesn't Daddy talk to Uncle Joe?" I asked, after observing at a family wedding reception that some of my favorite relatives were seated at tables at the opposite end of the banquet hall.

"If you were supposed to know, Miss Nosy Pants, we'd tell you," she answered, staring straight ahead.

Once I was peering through our venetian blinds watching all the public school kids walk past our house on their way to class. My brother, sister and I had the day off in honor of the Feast of the Immaculate Conception. "Why do mostly colored kids go to Ward School and only white kids go to St. Jerome's?" I wondered aloud.

"I suppose because they're not Catholic," my Mother said in a tone of voice suggesting I could be on my hands and knees helping her wax the kitchen floor instead of staring out the window.

Ignoring the hint, I persisted. "Aren't they worried about going to Hell?"

"I guess not. Go play."

"What's in a CONDEMNED movie that makes it bad?" I asked my friend as I searched The Motion Picture Ratings in *The New World*, the Catholic weekly newspaper, hoping to find a movie my parents would let us see.

"*Baby Doll* is a dirty movie--my Grandma said that's why it's a C," Janice confided, "but we're not supposed to be talking about that stuff. Don't even look at the Condemneds," she cautioned, "or we'll be in trouble."

After years of "don't be so nosy" and "mind your own business," hundreds of grimaces and rolling eyeballs, I came to believe that not only our living room but everywhere I roamed was a veritable elephant graveyard.

Would I never know why Uncle Salvatore lived in a hospital, what Uncle Gigi died from or why colored people lived two blocks away but never crossed Wentworth Avenue? Even Nancy Drew, my favorite girl detective, would have been hard-pressed to solve these mysteries what with every question stonewalled.

Years later, I could really relate to the rabbi who prayed at the Wailing Wall for a half century with no reward. "What does it feel like to pray for peace at the Wailing Wall for fifty years only to have your country in constant conflict?" he was asked. "It feels like I'm talking to a fucking wall," he said.

I sympathized with the rabbi but at least he'd never been subjected to the Sister Adorers of the Most Precious Blood. Trained as human walls to not recognize a straight answer if they heard one, they specialized in teaching a unique blend of God's Word and bizarre folktale.

As a student, I tried very hard to restrict my questioning to only those issues which truly baffled me since these harridans had no compunction about playing the 'God will send you to Hell' card to keep a student in line. There were times, though, where I just really had to take the risk and at least try to get some of this straightened out. I knew I couldn't get to the bottom of everything at once lest I be expelled as a "troublemaker" and shipped to the public school despite my being Catholic. I'd judiciously drop a question here and there.

"Sister," I asked when the coast seemed clear, "why would God punish a baby and send it to Limbo forever just because she died before she was baptized?"

"Sister, if your body must be buried in a consecrated cemetery in order to go to heaven, what happens to people who burn in fires? What happens if someone dies in the forest and an animal eats him? Does he go to Hell?"

"Sister, what happened to the Christian martyrs who were eaten alive by the lions in Rome? What if the lions left an arm or a leg? Would the arm and leg get buried? Would just the arm and leg go to heaven? Would God say, "I know all things and I know who you are even without your head. Come on in anyway."

I always had lots of questions and even more worries not just about the Coliseum and the Limbo babies.

What about my friend Catherine's mother who was getting divorced and going to Hell? Catherine said her mother told her it was better to go to Hell than stay married to Catherine's father. I said extra prayers for her at bedtime.

What about the boy across the street who was killed in a car crash the very same Sunday he slept through Mass? All the busybodies said his mother set the alarm clock for him but he'd turned it off. Did he turn it off deliberately and say, "The heck with it. I don't feel like going to Mass today"? Or did he turn it off thinking he'd just lie there for an extra five minutes and accidentally fall asleep? Big difference. One way he was burning for all eternity. The other way God might have shown him some mercy and he'd just have to make a stop in Purgatory before going to Heaven. How long would he be stuck in Purgatory? Oh, God. I hoped God didn't take that the wrong way--I mean, I didn't really mean *stuck*. I knew we were lucky to have Purgatory considering the alternative.

I prayed God understood I wasn't trying to be a smart-aleck. I just really needed more answers, but I was getting the message, albeit slowly, that asking made things even more complicated. Maybe I was supposed to stop with the questions and mind my own business. Maybe there were some things I wasn't supposed to understand. Maybe it was true that if I was supposed to know, they'd tell me.

I asked the priest about it in Confession but all he said was, "Bless you, my child, just believe." But believe what?

Fast forward to 2007. Cardinal Francis George announces at a press conference that the Pope has declared Limbo a thing of the past. "From now on," he declared, "Limbo will no longer be taught."

"Does that mean," an obviously pagan reporter had the nerve to ask, "that Limbo no longer exists?"

"I didn't say that," said the tap-dancing Leader of the Flock, "I said the Papal directive states that it will no longer be taught."

How many elephants can the Vatican hold?

Do you suppose one is named "Pedophilia"?

My God, how could that ever have happened?

INTERROGATING MY STUFF
Carolyn B Healy

Last year, my questions were all about why grief strengthens some people and weakens others. Before that, my questions were about how to multitask 24/7. This year, they are all about my stuff.

I used to move at least every five years. The usual young couple-upwardly mobile-growing family thing allowed me to upgrade from college apartment to rented bungalow to great duplex to actual own home. That took 10 years, and then began the parade of houses, all of it spanning three towns and another 10 years.

Stuff was never a problem back then. Each new place opened up new storage options, so any new item I acquired easily found a spot. Plus, with each move it was easy to jettison the things that had outlived their usefulness. It was a tidy self-cleansing process, kind of a regular stuff enema.

The trouble began 18 years ago just before Christmas, when we bought the current house, an across-town move from a much smaller one. We quickly stashed our stuff, hosted Christmas for the extended family and got on with family life. The next time I looked up, a couple of months ago, I was surrounded, hemmed in, trapped, drowning in extra stuff which occupied nearly every nook and crevice in this once roomy house.

To understand my issues, you have to understand my marriage, a good but not easy match. Without me, my husband would probably prefer life in a sterile box devoid of any decoration save a decanter for his bourbon, a copy of This Old Cub, his favorite DVD ever, and his big screen TV.

Without him I might have inched closer to hoarder heaven. His unwillingness to tolerate visual clutter has helped me contain most of mine to my home office where I covered nearly every square inch of wall space with meaningful photos, my collections of suns and moons, a wall cabinet filled with mementos from my parents' era, and well, you get the idea.

What he may not know and the casual observer would miss is that I also have stuff cleverly hidden in strategic locations elsewhere in the house – in antique trunks and painted chests, under the bed, and under the other bed. Meanwhile, he somehow gained custody of the upstairs closets where he can spread out his wardrobe so that each shirt has breathing space. He didn't pee on the boundaries of his closets, but he protects them like he did. My move was to seize the basement. And fill it. As the years went on, we reached this stuff stalemate until nothing new could enter the house without something old leaving.

We lived like that in relative harmony until we recently decided to redo my office and the room next door, our bedroom, and finally remove the aqua carpeting that had come with the house and the blue paint we had added in our first year here.

Right now, the painting is done, the walls a calm beachy tan color, the new carpet is on order and the rooms are completely dismantled. Which brings me to the point where my questions kicked in.

Carrying box after box, bag after bag and stack after stack out of that office, I had my moment of truth – my stuff was unmanageable. I had to do something different to recover my freedom, my space, my lightness of being. My stuff had taken on a life of its own, like a kudzu vine wrapping itself around everything in sight. I had to take control. I resolved that I would conduct this project like a move, questioning the right of each item to re-enter the room when I move back in.

I started with my books, which are relocating to guest rooms where they will provide a gracious background for visitors. They will have a happier life there on their own, and I can visit them whenever I want.

The rest of the process will be more difficult. The interrogation will go like this. Each item will have to answer three questions to get back in:

1. What do I need you for?
   Are you about the past, the present or the future?
   Given that, why do you need to stay?
   Is your appeal practical, emotional, or spiritual?
   And so what?
   Will I use you never, occasionally, all the time?

2. What do you say about me?
   Do you reflect my whimsical side, a sad or serious time, a quality I have, an opportunity I missed?
   What need were you to fill; do I still have that need?
   How do I feel when I see you?

3. Would I buy you today?
   Do you belong with me at this point?
   Is there something else that should have your spot instead?
   Is there someone else in the world who would love to have you?

Feeble answers like "But you've always had me," or "You'll never make it without me" just won't cut it.

I have two giant boxes, in the basement of course. One will be for donations, the other for my upcoming Museum of Things I Can't Stand to Get Rid of But Don't Need to See Every Day, another place I can visit if I feel the need. With this plan, I feel better already, sure that next year's questions won't have to have anything to do with my stuff.

Ultimately, figuring out which questions to ask when just may be the key to the life we all want. In my case, it is now too late, but I could use a do-over on some of my earlier efforts. Instead of asking how to better multitask, what if I would have explored how to become more mindful 24/7? Maybe that's what's coming next.

IT'S MOST TELLING...
Bernadette Adora

I gave up asking a long time ago. To explain: my daddy liked to recall a particular incident, one of many that happened when I was about eight or so. We were visiting family in Appalachia and thereabouts -- he was born and raised in Barboursville, Kentucky. My cousin, Patty, was with us on that trip. We had driven from Detroit to and through the Smokey Mountains and back again one summer; I loved every moment.

At some time during our vacation, daddy took us to a beach where we could enjoy the water and have a picnic afterwards. I believe, we were in North Carolina by that time or maybe it was West Virginia – the family was up the mountains and down into the valleys and all around those parts for a few weeks. With pride, daddy showed off that vast land, which he loved more than life itself. It was an afternoon of splashing around in the water when Daddy instructed Patty to show me how to swim. Patty was a pretty, chubby little girl with long, thick, wavy hair – Indian hair my mother called it. I, on the other hand, was short, skinny, and seriously afraid to get my hair wet --- you'd be too if you had to sit upright and perfectly still in your mother's kitchen with a hot iron sizzling and crackling overhead as your hair was pressed smooth, strand by strand. Nappy hair was a dreaded consequence back then of rain showers, water balloon fights, humid summer nights, settling back in the bathtub, and swimming. So I don't know if it was the water or the fact that she was doing it all wrong – of course she was doing it all wrong. I'd had a lesson or two earlier that summer, and I just knew. Besides, I hadn't asked her, not that I couldn't or didn't know how; it never dawned on me to ask. I was fine; this was my daddy's big idea – and my hair was already wet around the edges and moisture was seeping up under my water-proof swimming cap with every splash and dunk. It was then that I stopped playing around and explained to Patty, in no uncertain terms, how to teach me to swim.

Daddy stood nearby in the water only up to his ankles laughing as my mother prepared lunch far away from the water's edge. Mother told me later he had said that he knew I'd be all right in life and stated something like, "That girl is gonna be all right; we don't have to worry about her. She can't swim a lick, but she sure can tell somebody how to and how not to!" He got that right – and I've also come to realize why I became a woman, who tells – and yes, asks only when necessary. It was not a matter of being "bossy" or an issue of control; it was about having received permission to be myself, early on. I was often congratulated, expected to step forward when it came to matters of self, of self interest. I was given this gift from both my parents.

Then there is the matter of the community that helped nurture me. Back when, there were two kinds of girls out there: weak and strong - or - big and little. I was tiny in stature but I was a "big" girl, who wanted to grow up like the women all around me, strong women. The girls and women, who acted first and asked (maybe) later, were common place for me and mine. The women, whom I knew, were strong willed, determined know-it-alls, who could and would tell you everything you needed to know whether or not you needed that information. It was later, much later that I learned: we "tellers" can be a big pain in the butt! I have also discovered that telling can be a disguise for a fear of being thought less rather than more. It can be a cover-up lest our insecurities and our "little girl" within be known by all. Better wrong, dead wrong than weak is the motto here. Better a big girl pain-in-the-you-know-what than a little girl wimp.

Asking is an art form -- is humbling, where I come from. It's something one did in stillness with the Lord, mainly … "give us this day our daily bread…." But now, as a New Thought Christian, even the Lord gets instructions – daily bread is no longer a request, it is a statement, it is a sure thing. Mercy, me!

So while I think of myself as a big girl, a strong woman, if not a strong-willed woman, I have come with time to better understand the measure of this woman. Not unlike those beautiful hills of Kentucky, I have gone up my mountain and back down again to dwell in the valley below. I care about those who grace my life, and I have come to learn that I know no more and no less than anyone else – and still unafraid to tell you so; I may understand it differently is all. It is only now that I ask more and tell less. I ask out of caring; I ask out of respect; I ask out of knowing that I don't know – and that maybe one day I will get to that place of Knowing. Yet, I believe that should I arrive at that place, I won't need to tell and I won't need to ask because, I won't *need*. Now won't that be lovely?

But until then, I will continue to ask for directions, about the price of things, about your day, for the time, for an occasional day of peace and quiet, and for help when it is clear I can't get it all done alone. And most importantly, I will try and remember to ask those nearest and dearest, if it is okay for me to be a pain in the butt – once in awhile.

.

PASS THE PSYCHO-BABBLE, PLEASE
Ellie Searl

Early in our marriage, whenever my husband and I disagreed, we'd argue to the point of verbal warfare. There'd be name-calling, accusations, recriminations. Issues became cosmic. It took days to get beyond the bitterness and resentment.

I started many of the arguments masking my agenda in a cunningly intoned, *"I have a question,"* which set Ed's teeth on edge and put his guilt reflexes into high alert. He had learned that this was a loaded opener - the precursor to a kick-in-the-gut combat question: *"Why do you always . . . ?" or "How come you never . . . ?"*

I admit it was weasely to start trouble by announcing an accusatory question. I reasoned that hinting at a transgression gave Ed just enough lead time to marshal a generic defense, eliminating any need for a fight -*"Oh, I'm sorry for* (fill in the blank). *Did that cause a problem for you?"* Aside from this blame-eating reply, there were few responses I'd accept. He was wrong. I was right. Ed resorted to sarcasm, and I'd admonish him, tossing in belligerence and scorn for good measure. We became trapped in cyclical point–counterpoint condemnation.

These lose-lose fights left us exasperated and confused. Once we stuck pins into each other's balloons, we didn't know how to fix the holes. I'd develop a headache. Ed grew silent, very silent. It wasn't good. We needed a change.

It was during the late 70's – that period reeling from the aftermath of the Vietnam War - when Ed and I discovered improved ways of communicating. Our country was beginning to heal its civic wounds in the wake of national unrest. Conflict resolution and sensitivity training promoted by peace-not-war Flower Children trickled into the households of mainstream America. Haight-Ashbury hippies roused from their stupors, studied win-win communication, and sought employment with family health plans and retirement benefits. The Civil Rights and Women's Movements gained momentum, causing society to rethink the consequences of inequality, stereotyping, and sexist language. I-messages became popular. And we discovered the benefits of Carl Rogers' Client-Centered Therapy.

This non-directive approach to counseling entered our lives through a series of classes we took for our graduate degrees. Client-centered therapists aren't manipulative. They ask very few questions, and they don't tell their clients what to do, what to think, what to change, or what to believe. We appreciated that people in client-centered therapy could retain their dignity while focusing on uncomfortable issues such as hating their fathers or feeling inferior to their children. It was bad enough that people had to admit they were nuts. They shouldn't also be subjected to the intimidating strategies of an aloof psychoanalyst, writing interpretations on a notepad, making diagnoses, and offering condescending treatment plans based upon coerced answers to embarrassing questions. *"Hmm, mm. And how spastic are your bowels during these times of stress?"*

Ed and I realized we were pseudo-psychologists in our day-to-day relationship, scrutinizing each other, as though studying rat behavior in a lab maze. We interpreted and diagnosed. We bullied each other into acknowledging transgressions, and I connived my way into heart-to-heart, I'm right - you're wrong squabbles. But within client-centered therapy and a compilation of win-win, conflict resolution, sensitivity training, non-stereotyping language, and I-messages, we found a bag-load of resources to help us devise a new approach to everyday conversation.

We created a home-based, spouse-centered system of communicating. We'd respect each other's points-of-view. We'd keep our emotions stable, our feelings balanced. Our differences of opinion would be settled through negotiation, compromise, and productive decision-making. We'd be in Talk Heaven.

There were ground rules. No angry outbursts, no recriminations. No telling the other what to think or how to behave. No guilt trips. No accusatory questions. Keep it win-win.

So it began.

We expressed ourselves through courteous I-messages and acknowledged each other's feelings.

"I feel a little annoyed when the driver's seat isn't pushed back after you drive the car."

"I hear you, Ed. It sounds like your legs might get all scrunched up. I don't mean to cause you discomfort. I'll be sure to remember next time."

"Thanks, Sweets. I'm glad you understand."

We engaged in positive discourse through mutual respect and understanding.

"I feel somewhat neglected when you watch football all night."

"I hear you, El. It's good to know how you feel about my sports channel. When this game is over, let's pick a show to watch together."

"Okay, Hon. I'll read for awhile."

We implemented reflective listening strategies.

"I feel just a tad frustrated that we're moving so slowly down each aisle. I'm kind of anxious to get home."

"Thanks for expressing your feelings. I gather you'd like me to stop looking for so many labels. I'll try to speed up."

"Great, and to be honest, I kind of already know how much sugar I'm ingesting."

Feelings became clear.

"I feel really disappointed that you didn't come into the store with me. I could have used your help."

"Got it! I see it disturbs you that I might find it more enjoyable to listen to the radio in the quiet of the car instead of traipsing through the store with you again."

"You seem to understand. I hope you listened to something really interesting while I did all the shopping."

Feelings became very clear.

"It aggravates me that we came for a dinner party and now we're listening to some pitch to give money. I must have missed something in the invitation."

"I hear you. Apparently this charitable event upsets you."

"I should have stayed home."

"Good idea. Go home."

Feelings became crystal clear.

"Look, it pisses me off when I choose a god-damned station and then you go and switch the god-damned station to some other god-damned station that I don't want to listen to. I'm doing all the god-damned driving."

"I hear you, Ed.

"Of course you hear me, unless you've got shit in your ears."

There are times when abject failure tickles the soul. A giggle rose from my gut and burst through the grin I couldn't suppress. Ed snickered. We buckled into spasms of cleansing laughter.

We had been trying to enlighten our marriage by solving problems of the heart with intellectual gibberish and text book terminology. Our spirits had become lost in a quagmire of artificial I-messages and contrived reflective listening exchanges. Attempts to follow the rules had made us automatons reading from a stoic script written for witless actors.

Where was our intimate, spontaneous relationship with all its foibles and emotional turmoil? It was time to revisit good old arguing - with some modifications. We separated the pitfalls from the benefits of our new-fangled strategies. Dump insipid collaboration. Keep negotiation and cooperation. Dump the gravity. Keep the humor. Dump the pretense. Keep the truth.

Now, when Ed and I have a concern, we get right to the point. I don't start arguments with a sneaky *"I have a question,"* and we don't pretend everything is hunky-dory when we'd rather wring each other's neck. It's almost Talk Heaven.

Letting Go

Having Been Raised . . .

   . . . to love, listen, encourage, fix, advocate, counsel, accommodate, nurture, assist, correct, scold, teach, appease, advise, support, serve, feed, and protect, is it any wonder women have trouble letting go? Decades ago, girls were defined as good if they followed the rules. Today we know that following the rules blindly is self-limiting. For some of us, the painful consequences of holding on to old ideas help us let go. For others, trust in our own moral compass is enough.

NOT THE WORST WAY
Carolyn B Healy

The first time it hit me was a Sunday morning in April, the year my first-born son was a junior in high school. My husband and I were on our usual outing, grabbing bagels for the kids and time for coffee and conversation on our own. There was no hurry as both kids were still sprawled in their beds, sleeping the sleep of the adolescent - truly exhausted and deeply entitled.

We sat in the middle of Einstein's Bagels and idly discussed our recent college visits– the schools we could picture him adapting to, or not– when the earth tilted and I understood for the first time that he would really leave – and break up the happy home I had poured my heart and soul into for all those years. The tears started, right in front of anyone who chose to look, mine streaming and his only welling up. After minutes of trying to stop, I left, and stumbled out into the next phase of life – the Letting Go era.

I have snapshots burned into my memory documenting the journey from that moment to the actual goodbye –the swirl of red robes at graduation, heartbreaking trips to Bed Bath and Beyond for the essentials of dorm life, my son happily sorting through shower totes and bedspreads, me searching the eyes of other moms to see if they were adjusting better than I was.

Finally, the three of us drove to Brown, leaving a disgruntled younger sister at home to start the school year under Grandma's supervision. In a Cape Cod hotel lobby I witnessed a scene that said it all. A young mom was leaving for the airport, briefcase in hand, as her little boy followed with his dad. He called, "Mommy, here I am! Wait for me." He couldn't imagine that she was going without him. I could relate. My son put his arm around my shoulders and said, "Oh no. Oh Mom," with a chuckle, and shot his dad a helpless glance.

At the freshman dorm, when all the excuses to stick around were exhausted, we left. In the courtyard we passed another couple standing in a wordless embrace, the mom with her eyes closed, the dad clasping his arms around her. That scene held all the hopes and agonies of getting your precious child this far and having to step aside.

More stories came our way. There was the sixty-ish dad who tearfully recalled his son's departure fifteen years before, a mom who drove the long trip home because dad was too broken up, a new acquaintance who reminded me that there are worse ways to lose a child.

I know now that a river of inevitable grief runs just underneath family life, waiting for us to be tossed in. But 10 years later, having long ago climbed back out, I like this new era that I dreaded so much. My son is in Barcelona this week, my daughter the banker is coming out Thursday, and I am growing used to suiting myself rather than focusing on other people's needs. We will no doubt be thrown into that river again, but we are practiced now and can look ahead with hope to the rewards we can't see from here. Life is good, after all.

OPEN WINDOW
Bernadette Adora

Letting go is to allow for more. I honestly believe that resisting change, holding on can thwart our personal as well as our collective development. Letting go allows for peace of mind and a strengthened spirit when love is lost, abandoned, or even awakened. Letting go assists with shaping and refining our dreams whether they are sweet, bitter, or just phony-baloney; dreams are the stuff that helps deliver our daily bread be it a salty, bland, or fine loaf. There should be a letting go of the old and the worn-out, whether or not we ourselves brought it in from out of the cold.

The night of November fourth, two thousand and eight, I began letting go in earnest. The window swung open wider than I knew possible – not in my lifetime I had thought. But, it swung open nonetheless, and I began to let go and acknowledge dreams deferred; fears untold; and a deep, abiding despair inherited from those, who had loved me dear; mine, who would wish me safe, if only I could stay small enough, hidden somewhere out of harm's way. I am the great-granddaughter of a man, who survived the Klan when being sought through the back country in Georgia for being thought uppity and above his station in life. I am the granddaughter of a man, who was born a slave in the hills of Kentucky. I am the granddaughter of a woman, who stepped through the doors of a prestigious college only to clean homes of the rich until arthritis and old age took its toll, and she could no longer bend or kneel. I am the granddaughter of another, a midwife and nurse to folk denied the care afforded those with the proper birthright by color or caste. I am the great-granddaughter, granddaughter, daughter, mother, sister, niece, auntie, and cousin of teachers, a judge, bus drivers, politicians, nurses, lawyers, artists, government workers, machinists, salesmen, doctors, housekeepers, students, athletes, union members, housewives, soldiers, chief cooks and bottle washers!

"Sit up straight and carry yourself thus," I would tell my daughter when she was little. "You are descended from kings and queens." I taught her by word to be large, visible, and always in the right way, while I stayed smallish, somewhat hidden, and well, mostly out of harm's way – but not too much it now seems. Do as I say, not as I do – what a mixed message my daughter received. But as she moved forward with more courage in her young life than I ever dared, I continued to carry bags packed with deferred dreams, stuffed with fears yet to be told, and heavy with despair, which unbeknownst to me was going out of the first open window. The night of November fourth, two thousand eight, I began letting go.

And, yes, there still exists too much of the hatred and ignorance that chased after my great-grandfather nearly a century ago. And there remains the naysayer and the disheartened along with the madness and sadness of the human condition. My ancestors would caution me if they could in lowered voices with knowing shrugs and furrowed brows, all the while taking firm hold of my shirt sleeve to help spirit me away to a safer place. Yet, through a window opened wide, an odd assortment of old baggage floated up, out, and away on a November night. A new smaller bag replaces the old, where I have begun to add an immeasurable amount of trust in all things good. This is my bag that I open that I pack that I close that I pick up that I carry that I set down and that I empty at will; I respectfully discard those limiting ancestral patterns.

I am letting go of what no longer serves me or mine by embracing the present as one tiny conduit for tomorrow's today. I wish to welcome the descendents of all the kings and all the queens everywhere as a granddaughter, daughter, mother, sister, auntie, cousin, friend, neighbor – as one good woman amongst so very many!

GHOSTS IN THE DUST
Ellie Searl

I don't like to go into the basement and look at all my old, grimy stuff.

I have intended to phone 1-800-GOT-JUNK for months now. But there are some items in the basement that hold stories and are ripe with nostalgia. I can't part with these bits and pieces of history. I'd be throwing away the stories they hold.

Old-fashioned cross-country skis and boots, long ignored and covered in layers of soot, reminders of frosty afternoons in the Adirondacks, ski-skating over snow-covered pine needles and moss.

Two by fours haphazardly leaning against Ed's idle worktable where he fashioned our futon bed frame and Katie's bench with birds painted on the side. Rusted nails, bolts, varnish can tops, and a hammer head lay scattered in sawdust shavings and wood chips.

Mildewed board games with ripped cardboard tops stacked on make-shift shelves: Scrabble. Parcheesi. Monopoly. A French edition of Chutes and Ladders from when we operated the group home in Montreal, all covered in twenty-five years of cellar grunge, laundry lint, furnace ash, mouse turds, and dead flies.

Everything smells musty. It's too dirty to touch. But it's all too evocative to give away.

The boxes in the far corner are filled with crinkled age-old, yellowed newspapers protecting a set of dishes I thought I'd want way back at an estate auction when I was in my mid-thirties. Katie was a just little tot and played with her Dakin stuffed dog on the grass behind my chair under the auction tent. The house was full of things that used to be part of the family that once breathed life into the walls and furniture. Item upon item taken from the house and delivered to the auctioneer. Items left over from lives with the same set of hopes and dreams that probably abounded among the people under the auction tent bidding on the personal treasures and mundane, everyday paraphernalia that eased or confused or complicated the lives of WVS and his family. Picture frames, an oak sideboard, a grease-stained kitchen table, with matching ladder-back, rush bottomed chairs, a set of silver spoons with WVS engraved along the length of the handle. I could hear people wondering – what nationality was this family? German? Irish? Did the father rule with an iron fist? Did he terrorize his wife and children into conciliatory behavior? Or was there laughter and lamplight and love around that oak kitchen table as the children knocked over glasses of milk and dropped buttered bread upside down, letting grease soak into the wood grain?

Out came a set of hand-painted, rose patterned dishes, probably wedding dishes, probably the *good* china. I wondered what special meals were prepared to honor these, their company dishes. Did their family argue over who would carve the turkey? Did they have rare roast beef with Yorkshire pudding at Christmas? Did they serve family style? Or did Father dole out the food and pass the plates politely to his right? Did they serve lighter than air sponge cake and home-churned peach ice cream on chipped dessert dishes? Was there a baby crying somewhere in the house during dinner? Did Grandma insist, "Let me go, Verna, you just sit there and finish your meal. Put some meat on those bones." Did Grandma bring the baby back into the dining room and sit between Aunt Jewel and Cousin Agnes as they oohed and aahed over the sweet, precious thing - the spitting image of Grandpa? Did they say in rotation - "Why, just look at those eyes" and "It's the darndest thing" and "My,

104

my" and "Mark my words"?   Is that baby now a great-grandmother rocking aimlessly in some nursing home common room gazing at, but not hearing, "Wheel of Fortune" re-runs, waiting for a night-shift aide to come and take off her sticky supper bib?

I never used that set of dishes. Perhaps I just couldn't layer new stories of my life over those of this family. It would be like casting their life into oblivion. As long as these dishes remain packed in the very newspapers that were folded so carefully and gently around the fragile cups and dinner plates, then maybe their stories will stay alive somewhere in the minds of the long-ago children turned grandparent and great-grandparent.

And perhaps if I don't give anything of mine away and I let my basement possessions wait for some garage sale or estate auction, a young mother will wonder about me, making my life significant and real in her imagination while her little girl plays with dolls in the grass.

OUT OF RESPECT
Mary Lou Edwards

I've had my share of culture shock as I traipsed through Europe, the Americas and the Middle East, but nothing could have prepared me for my first encounter with a burqua clad woman on a flight from Rome to Beirut. Not pictures, not books, not stories—nothing could have prepared me for the searing image of the ghostly apparition.

A fastidiously groomed man in a Savile Row suit, Gucci loafers and a Rolex guided the ethereal shroud to its seat. Swathed head to ankle in a voluminous black cover replete with a plastic Darth Vader-like screen masking its face, it seemed like a character in "Night of the Living Dead."

When the meal was served, her gloved hands flipped part of her veil forward creating a mini-tent under which she ate. Except for her feet, you would never have known it was a person—no skin, no arms nor legs, no voice.

I was simultaneously fascinated and repulsed, though I'm not sure which part of the scene prompted my visceral reaction. After all, growing up with nuns exposed me to some very unusual attire, and I was steeped in a religion which routinely vilified women as "occasions of sin" so it wasn't as though misogyny was exactly foreign to me.

Maybe it was the proud, pristine peacock steering the faceless, formless figure down the aisle. Maybe it was the beautiful faces of their children knowing that, at puberty, the boys would become men while the girls were destined to disappear. Maybe it was the realization that a change in geography could make any woman, myself included, an erasable nonentity. Maybe it was the cheap jelly slippers that peeked from beneath the capacious black robe. Whatever it was, it overwhelmed my heart.

In Beirut, I shared the encounter with my Egyptian friend, Mohsen. "Ah," he explained, "we Arabs respect virtuous women—that is why we require the burqua."

Oh. My. God.

Years later, my daughter told me about helping to plan a 'Take Back the Night' rally on campus.

"Hundreds of students," she explained, "will protest violence against women. We're going to chant 'Yes means yes! No means no! However we dress, Wherever we go!' It's about victimization," she declared, "about empowerment, too. But really, Mom, I think it's about respect, don't you?"

"Yes, Lia, it is about respect," I replied, flashing back to the image tattooed to my soul so long ago. "Americans don't always get it right, but we do keep trying."

Write Impressions
www.writeimpressions.blogspot.com

Having the Last Word . . .
www.marylouedwards.blogspot.com

And Then . . .
www.elliesearl.blogspot.com

Apple Core
www.bernadetteadora.blogspot.com

The Inquiring Mind . . .
www.carolynbhealy.blogspot.com